Languages of Colour

Edited by Alexandra Loske

The Frogmore Press
2012

CONTENTS

The true colour of life is the colour of the body, the colour of the covered red,
the implicit and not explicit red of the living heart and the pulses.
It is the modest colour of the unpublished blood.

Alice Meynell, *The Colour of Life*, 1896

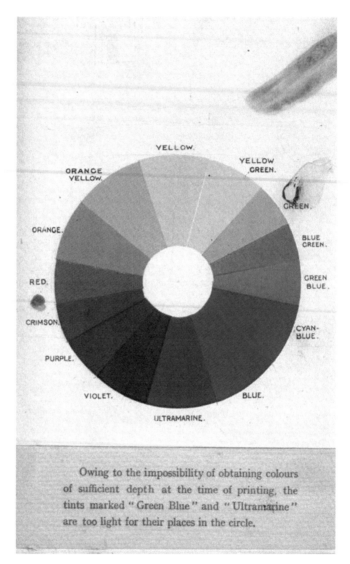

YELLOW.

YELLOW GREEN.

ORANGE YELLOW.

GREEN.

ORANGE.

BLUE GREEN.

RED.

GREEN BLUE.

CRIMSON.

CYAN-BLUE.

PURPLE.

VIOLET.

BLUE.

ULTRAMARINE.

Owing to the impossibility of obtaining colours of sufficient depth at the time of printing, the tints marked "Green Blue" and "Ultramarine" are too light for their places in the circle.

A colour circle from a 1915 colour handbook for painters and artists by H. Barrett Carpenter. The pasted-in slip underneath is evidence of the shortcomings of colour printing in the early 20th century. The paint smudges on the plate are signs that this manual was indeed used in a painter's studio, probably by the owner of the book, a D.R. Roper.

PREFACE

A few years ago I embarked on doctoral research into colour schemes and the use of pigments in historic interiors. During the course of my studies I was intrigued by the many different approaches and attitudes to colour and hoped I could gather some of these voices and publish them in some way. The idea for a very open and multi-disciplinary collection of writings and artwork on colour emerged. The response to the call for submissions was as varied in form and focus as I had expected, and more overwhelming than I had anticipated.

At the outset I had the rather naïve idea of organising the anthology neatly in the Newtonian order of rainbow colours. The originality of the submissions and the infinitely creative nature of both language and colour soon made it clear to me that this could not be achieved and that instead I should let the book express exactly this. So there is no division between fiction and non-fiction, poetry and prose, image and text, nor is there a chronological order. I have tried to let the pieces connect and speak to each other as seemed natural. The result is an anthology that includes pieces as diverse as an essay on a 16th century Italian colour dictionary, a personal memoir of the painter John Hoyland, who died while this book was being edited, a poem on the fear of yellow (*Xanthophobia*), musings on the wrong kind of blue in the sky of early photographs, notes from a library devoted to colour and two different translations of Rimbaud's famous colour poem *Vowels*. The collection is illustrated with a range of historical images and contemporary artwork, all of them, in my opinion, conveying the sheer joy of colour.

The title *Languages of Colour* was the working title, but it stuck. I chose it because I thought it expressed the many different ways of trying to explain, interpret and make use of colour. I later remembered that one of the most important contemporary writers on colour, John Gage, had given a chapter in his last book *Colour* exactly this title. Julian Bell had already contributed a shortened review of this book to this volume when we heard, in February 2012, that John Gage had died. The title is therefore even more poignant and in some small way a tribute to John Gage.

This book would not have been possible without the help, enthusiasm and generous support of many friends and colleagues. My particular thanks go to Neil Parkinson and the Colour Reference Library at the Royal College of Art for providing some of the most stunning historic colour images, and to Steve Pavey, who has contributed generously to the printing costs.

Howard Wright

IT WOULD BE

If air had a colour it would be green —
those interior shadows, the overhang
and crouching undercut banks; the heat
on the damp and grasping nettles.

If moon had weight it would be gold,
a sovereign moon on the rise,
spending itself on the motorway's roar
and a plane descending the poignant grey.

If language had a sign it would be red,
warning me what not to say
or to tell the truth differently
so it doesn't sound like a lie.

If river had metal it would be silver
and all that is childhood, its surfaces
and forms, memory's torture and time's
hygiene, the slow eddies and depths.

If love had wisdom it would be blue
and irreplaceable, and we would walk
to the viaduct and learn to be alone
because there is no wisdom in love.

Rachel Rooney

NOTHING

Red; it's overrated. See that token
red on a single stem, that
redness of me waiting like a pillar box.
Red's too easy.

Blue is foolish.
Blueness; I can dive right into it. Yes,
blue's an invite; it's the touch of tiles in a pool.
Blue. Don't do it.

Yellow's hell. Avoid it.
Yellowness is madness.
Yellow. Break it down and it's the sound it makes.
Yellow. I won't enter it.
.
Greenness; it isn't me.
Green is somebody else's smell and
green's their home, fingers, mould.
Green grows. Best keep away from it.

White? Now, that's more like it.
White's an absence. It's nothing and all I ever wanted.
Whiteness, pure and sweet as a fantasy.
White. I can almost taste it.

Graham Dean: *Small Funicular Station 2*, 2009

Alison Chisholm

SELF COLOUR

I am the palette where colour begins:
livid with lung and kidney, liver, heart.
I course with scarlet, draw it back
through indigo veins. Pale cream skin
envelops white of bone, maroons and browns,
brain's grey.

I look through blue and black,
see light that scatters, that regroups,
gives prismed shades to solid things,
gives empty space its abstraction.

I keep my secrets locked inside,
vital until death's dulling;
know that I
am artist's trio of red, blue, yellow,
additive combining of blue, red, green,
subtractive cyan, yellow, magenta.

James Goodman

PAINTING THE CLAY

white with a hint of gorse-tinder
white with a hint of machine oil
white with a rhododendron gloss
white with a hint of clay-rock canyon
white with a hint of peacock butterfly
on a glint of quartz

powder white and copper quarry-lake
poisoned mud white
creamy white with a hint of mica
quartz white with a hint of sky

white with a hint of clitter on the sea-ward moor
white with a hint of clatter of falling rocks
tiny white with a shadow of slow wing turning
bone white with a blush of clay marrow

gorse haze at dusk white
mud-white
boot-white
fading night white

white with a hint of Nanpean clay-dries
white with a hint of Foxhole mica-dam

white with a hint of what happened
up Chegwins Farm

Clare Best

TO FREDDIE, MY SON

I wish I could take you to Assisi
a night in June. I want to take you
to the place that took us in
dream-tired, all the way from the flat north,
no hope of finding a room.

Seventeen, hair long enough to toss,
but afraid by nightfall in a dusty square —
moths mobbing the streetlamp,
the last *panini* gone.
We'd sung all the songs we knew.

She came from stone,
led us through convent doorways to a cell:
two beds, black crucifix hung between.
Below the window's splintered sill
a chipped enamel washbowl,

a pitcher of cool water
bearing the sun's dark scent. We slept
in silent absolution, woke to gauze light
over blood-tiled roofs beyond the casement,
the shock of doves on red.

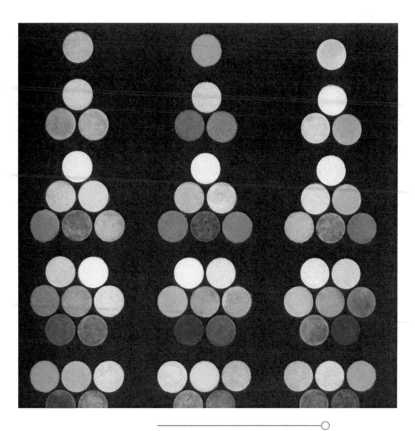

COLOUR REFERENCE LIBRARY

Background image from:
William Benson, *Principles of the Science of Colour*. London: Chapman & Hall, 1868.

14

Neil Parkinson

THE JOKER'S HAIR WAS SAP GREEN
Notes from the Colour Reference Library, Royal College of Art

The memory of painting a few colour wheels in A-level art lessons only takes you so far when you inherit responsibility for one of the world's largest collections of writings on colour. Spanning six centuries and containing almost two thousand books, the Colour Reference Library (CRL) at the Royal College of Art was one of my bigger challenges when I joined the RCA in 2006 to look after its various special collections. But one secret of rare books librarianship is that subject expertise is often only acquired on the job, at great speed.

At first, the names of the leading colour theorists whose work I quickly had to absorb rang only distant bells that struck the wrong notes. I thought of Goethe as a great playwright rather than a great colour theorist, while James Clerk Maxwell, in my limited frame of reference, was just the name of a big building at King's College London. But at some undefined moment the potentially vast and arcane world of colour studies became navigable and comprehensible. There was no initiation rite where all the facets of understanding coalesced, just repeated exposure and the need to field curveball questions from a constant stream of users (typically anyone from archaeologists to ad agencies). 'Which colours most appeal to children?' 'What are the universal meanings of pink?' 'How do you make a *new* colour?'

It is a measure of the ubiquity, and therefore almost invisibility, of colour, that only deeper immersion into the CRL has made me realise how far colour as a subject has saturated my life until now. Hitherto, its study or analysis seemed redundant, even in a life filled with the stuff. As an amateur portraitist from early teens, I dabbled with oils as I grappled with the vivid, if obscure, nomenclature of their hues (rarely do adjectives such as *alizarin*, *phthalo*, and *cerulean* pop up in ordinary discourse). Later I worked as a print designer, spending hours applying tints and shades to page layouts, and experiencing what I now know to be Munsell's famous three dimensions of colour – hue, value and chroma – as onscreen slider bars in image-editing applications.

The CRL challenged and expanded any unconscious knowledge I had accrued. Five years of exposure to split complementaries and successive contrast mean there is no return to a world where colour is merely present. I am in on its tricks. I know, for example, that the recent trend in film posters for an orange-and-blue scheme is an exploitation of simultaneous contrast to maximise impact. And although I cheerfully think of my favourite colour as *Naples yellow*, I am struck by Faber Birren's assertion in *Color & Human Response* (1978) that colour-preference tests universally demonstrate yellow to be the least popular of the six main colours. Nothing wrong with minority taste, of course, but, Birren notes, yellow rises up the preference ranks only 'among insane subjects'.

Perhaps my most enduring coloured memories are drawn from early exposure to the vibrant primary palettes of Marvel and DC comics, which transfixed me as a child of the 1970s and 80s. Working in the CRL prompted me to re-evaluate the colour schemes of the red capes, indigo cityscapes and luminescent laser beams which burned so much brighter in my youth on the yellowing newsprint than any additive colour emitted from the television screen. While obvious now, it had never occurred to me before, for example, that in a fantasy world of potentially limitless colour, the principal superheroes (including Spider-Man, Superman, Wonder Woman and Wolverine) are clad almost exclusively in interchangeable mid-tone subtractive primaries. Simple colour theory and symbolism could decode the colour scheme as resolute, indivisible, authoritative and universal: heroic qualities in spades. The history of colour printing would point to the economy of the flat-colour palettes and cheap ink formulae; psychology would reflect on the appeal of simple, bright colours to the children being enticed to part with pocket money, as I so willingly did, month after month.

But something strange is going on in the recent spate of big-screen adaptations of the comics I loved in my youth, which I would never have stopped to analyse in a pre-CRL life. In almost every case of chromatic costumed heroes, the value of the print colours has sharply decreased from earlier incarnations. The mournful *Superman Returns* (2005) features a costume visibly darker than the one first worn by Christopher Reeve in 1978. These are not the reds and blues of four-colour printing; instead, a peppercrumb of black has entered the mix. The same darkening afflicts principal costumes in film adaptations of *Spider-Man* (2002), *Daredevil* (2003) and *Iron Man* (2008). Bright colours connote authority on the page but on the screen risk appearing child-like and cheap, an embarrassment of certainty in a self-doubting, compromised world. ('What would you prefer – yellow spandex?' is the rebuke Wolverine receives in the first X-Men film, after expressing disdain for the team's standard-issue black jumpsuit. The joke for fans is that yellow spandex has served the character adequately in the comic books for decades.) It is no coincidence that these films are aimed at a broader, older audience. The CRL tells me that while children are traditionally drawn to bright colour, adults fall steadily out of love with it, and more suspicious of its connotations. Josef Albers's revolutionary series of visual exercises in *Interaction of Color* (1963) includes one in which students are presented with a wide swatch of reds and asked to pick out which in their judgement is the truest, reddest red. Albers found astonishing consistency of preference for one in particular: a mid-value hue we might call 'Coca-Cola red'. In simpler times we might also have called it 'Superman red'. Not any more.

One exception to this trend is conspicuous. The Joker in Christopher Nolan's gloomy Batman epic *The Dark Knight* (2008) is dressed entirely in vibrant secondaries: purple, green, orange. He leaps electrically from page to screen, all colours intact from his print debut seventy years earlier. This is all the more surprising given that Nolan has generally striven for a realistic tone in his Batman films, paring down comic-strip excesses for a cooler, hi-tech palette. Batman himself is monolithically black, and John Harvey's study *Men in Black* (1995) tells us plenty about how black uniforms relate to power shifts and unearned authority. But we should turn to David Batchelor's *Chromophobia* (2000), a wide-ranging and influential work that maps our ambivalent relationship with colour and the negative connotations of a vivid palette, for a clue to the Joker's appearance. Batchelor considers the notion of colour as contaminant, as a subversive outsider force: he cites the harlequin in Conrad's *Heart of Darkness* as a figure divorced from the orderly scheme of things, and whose colourful sewn-on patches are a badge announcing his very exclusion. Conrad's harlequin could be traded easily for the Joker: the gaudy wardrobe, the garish face-paint, are wilfully provocative, demonstrating autonomy from all the traditional monochrome power bases he undermines: the police, his vigilante nemesis, and the sharp-suited Mafiosi. In the film, the only visible compromise is his muted green-brown hair. Traditionally far more visceral and acidic in the comics, it should be nearer viridian than the production design's anaemic sap green. The green hair in the film has been described as a 'bad dye job', but this sounds like a rational explanation for the irrational; a misguided attempt to integrate subversive colour and tame the anarchy by reducing a perverse and wilful act to a mishap. My initial fanboy grumbling on first seeing *The Dark Knight* ('the Joker's hair wasn't green enough!') can be accommodated by the theory tucked away in the CRL: simply put, not green enough equals not mad enough.

In five years, I have learned that the study of colour can take many forms; its order, patterns and effects can be explained with words or images, with precision or speculation, analysis or intuition. Artists and designers embrace or reject its contents: those who visit the Colour Reference Library can have their practice challenged, up-ended, or reinforced. One person's insider knowledge is another's spoilers, as apt to dampen the creative process as to enhance it, and many prefer to speak the language of colour with disregard for its grammar. Perhaps it is best to see the CRL, its interdisciplinary contents and application, as a toolkit, or a utility belt: it provides a range of approaches to cultural analysis which often yield associations and interpretations hitherto dimly understood only on a subconscious level. It provides ways in to colour in any imaginable context, fostering deeply subjective, interpretative approaches, but anchoring these to observable phenomena and the laws of science. It is a parallel language, a decoder ring, and a cipher disk, to mark and interpret nothing less than the world before us.

Elizabeth Barrett

THE COLOUR-BLIND MAN

thinks of her hair the shade of raw silk
blowing like marram grass into her eyes.
He wants to gather it up in his hands,
hold it for her while she runs – his fingers
would twist knots at the nape of her neck,
braid ropes of light down her back.
He makes a detour on his way to work,
scans the store directory for *Haberdashery*.
The display is arranged as a colour wheel —
he picks a spindle from each section
of the spectrum — thinks of her running,
trailing a scumble of streamers in the wind.
He wants to pick the colours which match
her favourite things, complement her eyes
and lips, but isn't sure which each shade is.
At ten o'clock, where red-blue hues should be,
he sees in greyscale: oyster, pearl, ash.
He wants purple — hazards on the charcoal.
Next he selects a dove grey - compares it
in his memory to the box of shell buttons
she sewed on her dress. *Lilac*, she'd told him.
At the counter he hands over the reels —
asks for a metre of each. He imagines her
pulling them from the bag one by one -
Vanilla he will tell her. *Chestnut. Sky Blue.*
And this? *Apricot.* What about these two?
He will distinguish their red-blue hues.
And how will he call this? *Mulberry* he thinks —
to hold back her hair the shade of raw silk.

Michael Swan

CHARCOAL BLACK, ROWAN RED

Charcoal black, rowan red,
in a twelvemonth I'll be wed,

falcon's claw, weasel's tooth,
if my lover tells the truth,

bird's throat, cat's ear,
but her words are false, I fear,

cold blade, viper's bone,
and I shall live my life alone,

saffron yellow, amber gold,
till the day when, sick and old,

I take that road where none comes back.
Rowan red, charcoal black.

Nisha Woolfstein

THE IMPURITY OF GLASS

Extracts from a novel

Red: The Queen's English

The most interesting thing in the room is his red wallpaper. It is a deep and fading crimson, the colour punctuated by a repeated scene of identical Chinese fishing boats returning home – if the tiered and richly decorated pagoda, standing at the edge of etched and linear waters, is their home at all. Marta is squeezed on the low-slung sofa. It will be some months before she first hears Mr Gander say, 'If these walls had ears, my! If these walls had ears…' But it will make perfect sense to her: of course these walls would have dozens and dozens of ears, all those Chinese fishermen listening, rowing, listening. Chairs, which are arranged all around the room, now seems themselves a collection of boats in a floating market place; each one different, mismatched, bearing its floating cargo of variously shaped women.

Mr Gander sits in a high-backed armchair to the left of the tiled fireplace. The word seems ill-equipped to describe the function of this object, as there had not been a fire nor the semblance of one in its grate for many years. Instead, the heat of the room smoulders gassily from a rickety heater tucked in front of the sideboard. The place where the fire would once have been is referred to as the 'Altar', and holds a large, now fading, picture of the Virgin Mary. To the right of the fireplace, Dr. Cynthia sits like a wooden doll upon her chair, with such familiarity that, had Marta not been accustomed to visiting Cynthia in her own home, she would have been sure that the chair — and perhaps the house too — was Cynthia's very own.

Beyond the curtains, the street is softly dark with the warming of April evenings. But from the foggy air of the sitting room, the ordered candles lined in their brass holders along the redundant fireplace — reflecting and multiplying in front of a cut-glass mirror — give the illusion of eternally impending Christmas.

'…and that's when Those in Authority are able to lift us up, to reach towards the higher planes…'

Cynthia's voice is the ticking of a clock, marking time, setting its boundaries. A thin woman sitting next to Marta's mother is playing with a chain around her neck. Perched on one of the chairs brought in from the kitchen and spare-room, the woman seems unnaturally at one with a skittish spider plant exploding from the sideboard behind her. She notices Marta watching her and smiles suddenly, a distracted smile, like the flaring of a match. A curvy woman in a voluminous white dress sits beside Marta on the sofa. Her long waves of red hair have softened the ageing of her face, so that at first glance she looks young, but she isn't. To her other side, smart, high-heeled shoes sit neatly beneath a cheerfully sun-tanned woman in a matching skirt and jacket.

Cynthia stops speaking now, while Vaughan Williams is put carefully onto a record player in the corner of the room. As if she too were the record, Cynthia seems to start up talking again just as the music begins.

'Now we close our eyes and feel the impulse of Master ... taking us to the Sudan...'

Each of the women closes their eyes. The Lark Ascends. Why does Marta sit there with her eyes open, hardly even aware that she is the only one who hasn't closed them? She looks from one woman to the other; looks again at the Chinese fishermen in their little boats; looks across to a glass-fronted cabinet, where books, photographs and objects are equally unreadable in candlelight; looks towards Mr Gander, and sees without surprise that his eyes are not closed but looking around the room. Eventually, they rest upon her. She looks away, closing her eyes, but she still sees the tumultuous leaves of plants grappling with the space around them. Forests continue growing behind her eyes. Over time — months, years — the image of these plants will become fixed at the back of her eyelids, but not yet. They are not yet moulded into a solid form, together with the armies of Chinese fishermen, and the notes from the record as it spins.

She tries to think about the Sudan, as Cynthia has said. She imagines a wide sand-duned desert, large, empty heat, and babies with rope-thin limbs and bulbous stomachs. Cynthia talks on. She has a soft, though not quite gentle, voice. She speaks the Queen's English, as it is supposed to be spoken. But the words seem to fall from her mouth like powder. Dust. Time wears on and, as the record is changed again, so eyes open again, and then shut. Even Marta's fascination with the lives of Chinese fishermen begins to wear as thin as the wallpaper itself, and the novelty of being the only child amongst a group of adults engaged in something unusual begins slowly to lose its promise.

'We know what this music symbolises.' Mr Gander's voice jumps in unexpectedly, sounding like a large and surprised goose as the opening bars of Rachmaninov, *Piano Concerto No. 2*, hum into life. 'The Golden Age. The missing link we have all been searching for.'
Feet shuffle. He is getting up from his chair, pushing himself vertical by its wooden armrests in a movement which must itself contribute to the wood's muscle-like sea-shine.

'It symbolises pure love. The love of long ago. Sweetheart...'

He gestures down at the girl in the middle of the sinking sofa and the room full of women stirs into life like a sleeping clutch of ducks. A brief, chaotic process of chair swapping ensues, which to Marta — by now far away with Chinese fishermen and Sudanese starvation — seems to involve everyone in the room. In fact it only involves three people.

Now, settled again, her mother sits between Dorothy and the billowing white woman upon the sofa. Mr Gander sits next to the spider-plant woman who plays even more with the pendant around her neck. And Marta sits in Mr Gander's armchair, across the deity-filled hearth from Cynthia, from where she feels as if she is suddenly on a stage. The star of a play. But where is the script? What are the lines? Though she is tall for eight years old, still her feet only just touch the floor, and the back of the chair rises high behind her. The women seem further and further away, as if pulled by the nets of the fishermen back to a shore, while she is in a new boat, not her own, cut loose and drifting deceptively fast in the unseen current.

'There you see. Purity.' He continues. 'The future of this Concept. Right here.'

And now Marta does close her eyes properly. Not because she has any intention of reaching the higher aeroplanes of which Cynthia seemed to have been speaking, but for at least three other, different, reasons: because of the embarrassment which washes over her like pink waves; because she has a feeling that somehow she has just tricked these people into something; and because she feels that the music rasping from the record player as it builds its emotion up and up again, might, if she is not very careful, actually make her cry — which seems the most stupid and embarrassing trick of all.

White: Lingerie

A grey day, a non-descript, season-less day. It feels a strange thing for a nine year old girl, going off in the small blue car of her family doctor, on a shopping trip. Parking the car in town, they walk onto the high street, the doctor's spongy grey hair bobbing beside her. Dr. Cynthia's skin suggests that she has been made of plaster, a mould for something missing.

They enter Debenhams. It is a busy afternoon and the corners of shopping bags prod Marta's sides as she squeezes amongst lines of women's clothes. Air conditioning pumps the claustrophobic smell of new carpets, in, out, in, out, and the shop breathes as one.

They reach a corner, crammed beside the ladies' changing room on the second floor. The women's lingerie section. Shopping for pants, with her mother, is a simple case of picking a set of children's briefs, the ones packed five together in a plastic box, cotton of course, sometimes in all different colours, or with stripes, flowers. Once, embarrassingly, with pink elephants. Simple childish pants. But she is not with her mother; this is a new and different business. Today they are buying secret underwear. Pure underwear. And it must all be white, nothing whatsoever but white.

She tries on knickers made of discreet satin, little bits of lace along the edges. These knickers come one-to-a-hanger. They pick three pairs, one French style, two bikini-cut. It takes a little while to find a pair of white tights. There are woollen tights, school tights, thick ribbed tights in blue, cream, red. Beige tights like ancient skin. Eventually a shop assistant points her checked polyester sleeve to the *special wedding tights,* 'the only small white tights we've got in stock at the moment I'm afraid.' Instead of a simple label above the plastic window of the box, these tights have doily white letters on a confetti-strewn, lilac blue background. They pass rows of brassieres; objects from a strange land of adults, not the land of girls with nipples like ladybirds. Cynthia picks out two vests; one cold, slippery, thin-strapped; the other clinging, thermal, lace-edged.

At the counter, phantoms of school friends appear across the crowded shop, becoming strangers in a double take. The whole shop seems like a giant chink between the curtains; the threat of crossing thresholds between worlds. She tries to blend in with the clothes hanging limply on the rails and feels such a fear of being found out, as if buying white underwear was a crime. Of course she is faintly aware that it is not a crime at all; it is only lingerie. Still, she will never mention the shopping trip, when she arrives home to her family for dinner.

Katherine Lubar: *Negative Light Patterns*, 1999

Megan Hadgraft

THE COLOUR THEORISTS

Phil was chatting away, and I was pretending to listen, when I suddenly realised all the other people in the room were looking in my direction. I said as charmingly as I could, 'Can I help you?' An American with perfect teeth said, 'We were just discussing the color of your dress.' I could actually hear the u missing from the word colour as it came out of his mouth.

'My dress?'

'The color of your dress. Is it pink or purple? I'd say pink, but these guys are telling me it's purple.'

They all looked at me expectantly. I could feel my face turning the same colour as my dress. I said, 'Actually, it's fuschia.'

The American laughed.

'May I ask why you're having this conversation?'

'May I ask?' He mimicked my accent. 'Sure. It all started because of my shirt. What color would you call this?'

'Blue. Midnight blue, to be exact.'

'Phil, what color is my shirt?'

'Well, I reckon blue, too.'

'See, to me it's purple. These guys think Allison's dress is purple, and my shirt is blue, but to me, Allison's dress is pink, and they disagree.'

Phil said, 'Maybe your shirt could be indigo, halfway between blue and purple.'

'You Brits. Allison's dress isn't pink or purple, it's fuschia, and my shirt isn't blue or purple, it's indigo. What color's your shirt? Got a fancy name for black?'

'This, my friend, is slate.'

'I love a man who knows his colors,' said the American. 'That's not at all gay.'

'I'm very in touch with my feminine side.' Phil put his arm around my waist and squeezed a bit too hard. 'But as I recall, indigo isn't a colour at all. It was invented by the Catholics, so the rainbow would have seven colours, not six.'

'Really? Is that a fact?'

'It could be fiction. I'm not really sure. It was something my chemistry teacher told us at school, and I've never verified the fact. It could be what you lot would call a load of BS.'

'Bullshit is the word you're looking for. Hell yeah. Got any interesting info on fuschia Allison?'

The only thing that sprang to mind was a rather iffy joke my former flatmate had told me, along the lines of: *What's the difference between pink and purple? — Depends how hard you hold it.*

I smiled to myself, then saw the astonished looks on the faces around me, and realised I had told the joke aloud.

'Oh dear,' I said. 'I think that may have been my danger glass of wine.'

Phil looked confused. 'I don't get it.'

'You've got your whole life ahead of you.'

The midnight blue American smiled as he reached for a bottle of white to refill my glass.

Peter Dunsmore

Ridiculous to wait for rain and sun.
A cube of Perspex and a table lamp
Instantiate the seven at a click.
Now you may find the missing shade of blue.
Below the red, beyond the violet
Only the void. Don't be deceived. It's there
We see, unseen, in darkness: there we burn.

Helen Overell

THE SHEDDING OF SEQUINS

A glint of pink on gold,
an insubstantial purple
circle, a deep blue disc,
all small as flung stars,
a tumbled trawl of light;

as though a mermaid swims
between these walls each
night in depths of air more
mountainous than an ocean
swell on a deep-bed trench,

her tail clad in iridescent
scales in every shade of sea;
far more than are needed
here in these white rooms
and so some fall, drift,

settle down; a round eye
winks from the windowsill,
while a cross-eyed stare
tilts from the floorboards
where a glance in a burl

looks out from a world
green with shifts of tide
that skim sky, bruise land;
I could be driftwood cast
aside, a figure in a dream.

Yugin Teo

KILIM

We poked our noses around the entrance of the carpet and kilim shop on a quiet street in the Turkish seaside town, grateful for the shade on blisteringly hot day. As our eyes adjusted to the dark interiors, we noticed an unusually quiet and reticent shop owner. Once accustomed to the lighting of the shop floor, we were greeted by walls decorated with carpets and kilims of varying sizes, designs, and textures.

Our eyes were drawn to a stack of small-sized kilims in a corner. Sensing our interest, he pulled out kilim after kilim, displaying the unique patterns and colours of each one before laying it down on the floor. The owner painstakingly described the provenance of each rug to us. Zigzagged lines and shapes, angular geometric patterns and symbols that were distinctive to the artistic traditions of each kilim-producing family. A language of blessing, protection, or fertility; one that was only ever fully known by the weaver.

I took my eyes off the kilims on the floor for a moment to scan the room, soaking in the warm colours on display: vermillion, crimson, burgundy, burnt umber, ochre, amber, teal, viridian, cobalt blue. My mind recalled an article concerning natural dyes used in kilim production in Anatolian art. The muted tones of natural dyes (reds from madder root, blues from true indigo, yellows from safflower) were conducive to a harmonious blend of colours that would otherwise clash.

We explained to the owner our past links with Turkey. Eyes lit up, he became noticeably more at ease with us. He reached under the table and proudly pulled out two well-worn photograph albums of his travels across Western Europe and North America. Alone, in a large yellow van, he had peddled his wares of Turkish carpets and kilims to the West. I imagined him taking the colours of Anatolia with him everywhere he went. The soft tones from the natural dyes, together with the textures of woollen yarns flat woven using centuries-old techniques, forging the ties of friendship evident in these old photographs.

We finally settled on one of the kilims on the floor, one of a pair from the same family of designs in Kayseri, Central Anatolia. In many ways the simplest in design, but with colours that spoke of our recent experiences travelling on the Aegean coast. The varying hues of blue across the flat woven surface recalled the crystalline waters of the Aegean on a cloudless day out at sea. Ochre and teal triggered memories of the arid landscapes of Ayasoluk Hill in Selçuk whilst climbing the ruins of St John's Basilica. The reds evoked the contrast of poppies growing amidst the ancient remains of Ephesus, the glorious cherries sold in fruit stalls on market days, and the ubiquitous çay we drank everyday.

We arrived at a price for the kilim. As he wrapped it in a tight parcel I couldn't help but feel an encroaching sadness, as our visit to the shop came to an end. We would soon be leaving Turkey, and the colours and smells of a recent experience were already receding into the past, into memory. As we left the old town I tightened my grip on the meticulously wrapped package in my hands - a visual and tactile reminder of Anatolia.

Catherine Smith

XANTHOPHOBIA

That summer, the celandines rampaged
through flowerbeds. The stains
on the gardener's hands where he'd
pulled them up by the roots. His palm
across my mouth.

Today in the supermarket, I saw all those
little suns trapped in the big freezers.

It made me cry and people stared.

A man with a green badge was kind.

But then, the ambulance, with its
weeping, the gash of yellow along
its side; I couldn't stop shaking.

The psychiatrist had fat purple veins
in his hands and neck, and a red pen,
a black notebook with blue lines.

He asked about the celandines - they always
do - but I know he wanted to whisper,
What colour knickers are you
wearing? You have to be on your
guard in these places. Any moment,
some bastard could pin you down,

hold a plucked flower under your chin.

Clare Crossman

THE COLOUR
(after a photograph by Gertrude Käsebier, c.1907)

Those winter afternoons when we walked
the river, you showed me the elements,
the sky. You kept a book of leaves and feathers
drawn from the fields you crossed,
saw shapes as blossom imprinted on the air.

You said there were too many gods to wonder
about one: concerned with essences,
for you there was fire at the heart of space.
We made sculptures from tree roots,
to be found before they were washed away.

Last January when the sky was every shade
of grey, black water on the road, furrows
like frozen sea, I took the photograph
you sent me from its frame. *The Magic Crystal (1907),*
all silvered black and white.
The girl in the beaded dress leaning to look
into brightness just before the shutter fell.

Your inked words on the back still
held you in their glancing: how your
ring turned to charcoal in the dusk,
your love of flight, the times we stood
together at the weir.
We meet in silence when we remember,
the material world is too full of possession,
it's natural to part.

But I believe you still walk on the other side of me,
as you did when we came home through
the window lit streets, when you said to
name the stones, let wildness speak.
We make our own path on the journey
towards night, the peony blooms,
each heavy petal falls, time shortens,
shade defines the light.

Kevin Bacon

BLUE SKY THINKING:
Early photography and a troublesome tone

Think of a nineteenth century photograph.

Then think of a colour that defines it.

It's likely that your imagined or remembered photograph is formed from the brownish range of hues commonly called 'sepia'. If not, you may have thought of the polished silver of a Daguerreotype or the dull grey of a tintype or collodion positive. But unless you have thought of a cyanotype, the photographic process originally used for the reproduction of 'blueprints', you will probably not have thought of the colour blue. Yet blue was the colour that made early photography possible, and the colour that defined its limits.

Until the development of panchromatic materials in the early twentieth century, photography saw very little of the world. The photochemistry of the day relied on compounds that were sensitive to a narrow area of the electromagnetic spectrum: from visible blue light through to invisible ultraviolet. Early photographers assiduously courted the magical properties of blue light, and this is amply demonstrated by Brighton's first photographer, William Constable. Constable, one of the first photographers in England to acquire a licence to use the Daguerreotype process, established a south facing studio overlooking the seafront promenade. Here, on cloudless days, he could enjoy light passed through a blue sky and reflected from a blue sea. This was enhanced by the windows and glass roof of his studio, which were adapted to tint the light a deeper blue. Although formally known as the Photographic Institution of Brighton, Constable's studio became popularly known as the 'Blue Room'.

But what blue light gave, it also took away. The chemical bias towards blue caused particular problems for landscape photography. Look at Victorian photographs of fishermen or holidaymakers on beaches and you will notice a recurring phenomenon. A favoured composition of a beach scene is to look towards the sea, capturing the focus of the shot in the foreground. Yet once a sufficient exposure time has been allowed for the people or details in the foreground, the blue sky and blue sea behind become overexposed. The sea and sky often become reduced to a pale, slightly eerie emptiness.

One solution to this problem was the use of multiple negatives. Often called 'combination printing', this technique is usually credited to the French photographer Gustave Le Gray. In the late 1850s Le Gray created a celebrated series of seascapes in which the sky and sea had been photographed separately using differing exposure times. Le Gray's prints were created using both the negatives, allowing tonally accurate images of both the sea and the sky to be assembled in a single print.

As a solution to a practical problem, Le Gray's method was ingenious, and its influence can still be seen in digital techniques such as high dynamic range imaging (HDR). Yet it also introduced an inherently realist medium to the possibilities of fakery. William Henry Fox Talbot famously described his photographs as having been produced by the 'pen of nature', but Le Gray's methods encouraged manual intervention in this process. It was a technical achievement with a creative legacy: at its best, it can be seen in photomontage, and the ambitious compositions of nineteenth century Pictorialists; at its worst it was exploited by unscrupulous spirit photographers, who claimed they could conjure images of the dead through their cameras.

But the dividing line between a practical solution and a creative embellishment is often thin. The Royal Pavilion and Museums holds one photographic print of the Pavilion that demonstrates this. Produced around 1910, it is a view of the building taken from the south side of the estate. At first glance, it is not an unusual view of the building, which had been a favourite of photographers since Fox Talbot first captured it in the 1840s. But take a look at the sky. Do those clouds look a little too low in the sky? And do the areas around the central minarets appear peculiarly pale?

Adolphe Boucher (attr.): *The South Gate of the Royal Pavilion, Brighton,* c.1910

This photograph is one of several in an album that are believed to have been taken by Adolphe Boucher. Born in 1869, Boucher was the son of a successful Brighton photographer and artist, who ran a studio in Ship Street from 1870 until his death in 1875. Boucher followed his late father into photography, but operated a studio in Twickenham. He seems to have made several trips back to the seaside town of his childhood, and this photograph is a result of one of these excursions. It is one of only two photographs in the album that contain a detailed sky; the others feature the pallid void typical of photographed skies of the time. So why did the Pavilion merit this embellishment?

One obvious answer is that Boucher was particularly pleased with this image, and wished to enhance its dramatic appeal. Then, as now, the Pavilion was Brighton's most iconic building, and he may even have considered the photograph to have commercial value. But it is tempting to think that Boucher may have been inspired by the building itself. With its Mughal exterior and intensely coloured Chinoiserie interior, the Pavilion is an unabashed fantasy, its clash of visual cultures driven by the romantic pretensions and imperial aspirations of King George IV (1762-1830). Although it had long ceased to be a royal palace by the time Boucher produced his photograph, the eccentric grandeur of the building continued to enchant sightseers, as it does today. But much of its charm and vigour derives from the colours deployed in its design; the challenge for the photographer was to reproduce this in a monochrome image.

Boucher's solution was to look to the skies, and be artful with the azure. A fine and early example of blue sky thinking.

Tamar Yoseloff

ILLUMINATION

Gold leaf, cadmium, ochre, saffron —
indelible once set on vellum.

The monks ground azurite and lapis
for perfect blue, took care

to cleanse their hands of poison
that made words sacred.

We place our fingers against
each other's lips, a vow of silence,

sense the touch mark even after.
I am brimming with words

but none can hold that moment
when our faces, edged in gold

glinted in the water's mirror,
the invisible sun within us —

so I let them fly, lead white
against a white sky.

Liz Rideal

DANZANDO CON BORROMINI, DANCING WITH BORROMINI

It was with the intention of studying Bernini and his drapery that I went to Rome. However, on a visit to the Palazzo Barberini I discovered Borromini's elegant twisting helicoidal staircase and was immediately seduced by the fabulous sense of space; the swirling oval gradation embodying a feeling of utter balance and exquisite form.

I decided to experience Borromini's architecture within the city, and to animate it with my drapery, using cloth and colour to highlight the spatial ambiguities of his work.

Borromini's restrained decoration, unique interpretation of architectural language, and his mathematic logic become the perfect foil for the subtleties of the ephemeral, richly coloured transparent silks that billow and twist with sublimated sexual energy. The gauze veils and reveals details of his buildings, and tantalisingly implies the human presence, evoking fleeting figures and a variety of emotional states. The chaotic movement of the drapery contrasts with the deliberate grace of Borromini's details, while the rich colour complements his white, space spaces. The resultant digital colour inkjet prints were shown together in Rome in September 2010, a year after I had been at the British School at Rome as the Wingate Scholar.

Liz Rideal: *Danzando con Borromini*, 2009

Liz Rideal: *Danzando con Borromini*, 2009

Jeremy Worman

FRAMED

On the threshold of the Friends' Room at the Royal Academy I felt the London winter sales crowds pulling me back to the streets. Inside, a group of well-dressed women discussed the merits of the exhibition. Around the walls of the Friends' Room, a vivid display of paintings and drawings, with bold Fauvist backgrounds of primary colours, highlighted the almost-undressed Asian men and women. The county ladies, in their quietly-pastel tweeds, remained unruffled by this display of eroticism. The women sank on to the dark leather sofas. The polished mahogany tables glowed with innate dignity. The hands of the county ladies were relaxed as they sipped their coffee, and I looked at their well-applied make-up and calm unblinking eyes.

A band of light crossed my eyes, from a thin brass strip, which stretched across the top of a black patent leather handbag from one of the women opposite.

I smiled at the proud, elderly woman, her white hair perfectly coiffured and lightly permed. She turned away, revealing her long neck and suggesting the posture of a horsewoman. She looked at her friend: 'I shall be in Wiltshire until June.' A green enamelled brooch, of two birds, sparkled on her shoulder. Her bag was now resting diagonally across her lap.

I smelt perfume – my mother's perfume – and her gloved hand seemed to reach towards me from the sofa. I closely observed the woman's bag, which was the same kind as my mother used to like. I could see my reflection in its black patent shine.

'You've dropped your powder,' I said as she got up to leave.
'Thank you so much.' She picked up the compact.
The pressure of the sales crowds no longer tugged me. I imagined the woman putting down her handbag in the quiet of her house, my image embossed upon it.

Niki Fulton: *Pastels on a Plate*, 2011

"Three dimensional blocks of colour are a helpful starting point when selecting a palette as the colours can be seen on different planes in both light and shadow, and can be moved around easily to create numerous colour combinations." Niki Fulton

Julian Bell

JOHN GAGE, *COLOUR IN ART*

I have been reading the last of John Gage's books, *Colour in Art*. Gage's achievement, here and in the 1993 *Colour and Culture* and its 1999 successor *Colour and Meaning*, was to tinge colour with time like no writer before. His curious and scrupulous mind teased out countless new nuances in our experiences of visual art. The insights Gage offered sprawled in all directions, from classical antiquity to Aboriginal culture, from heraldry to neurology to the colourman's trade, and it is hard to delineate a single theme that dominated his investigations. But in this volume, the centre ground is occupied by modernism, and the various hopes that 19th- and 20th-century artists invested in colour.

When was colour? Should we think back to the passion of postwar Americans for acrylic and metallic surfaces, for 'keeping the paint as good as it was in the can', in Frank Stella's phrase? Or to the trenchant insistence on primary red, blue and yellow in the interwar modernisms of Mondrian and the Bauhaus? The usual consensus is to place colour's prime in the forty years from 1880, the era when chemistry's heftiest products came forward to dominate the canvas: cadmium yellow, alizarin crimson, viridian, cerulean. A clamour of innovators - Gauguin, Van Gogh, the Fauves, the Expressionists, Kandinsky - were all pitching in to intensify colour experience, to subsume all other aspects of art within it, to charge it up with spiritual content.

Their initiatives form the dispersed highlights of Gage's text, which is organized by theme - colour in relation to psychology, language, shape, etc - rather than by chronology. The period is one of art history's most heavily worked veins, yet approached from these angles it still yields riches. What fabulous chimaeras they chased after, back then! In the wake of Baudelaire dreaming up his 'correspondences' of colour and sound, artists began to cherish the notion that every kind of sensory input might converge, so as to pitch participants onto some indefinable plane of transformed consciousness. Synaesthesia became a sign of spiritual election. Scriabin's colour keyboard of 1911, each key triggering a different hue to be projected in a melody-dependent lightshow, may be the best known synaesthetic extravaganza, but, as Gage drily records, the Russian composer was forestalled twenty years earlier by a Symbolist production of *The Song of Songs* at Paris's Théâtre des Arts:

> The opening scene, presenting the meeting of King Solomon and the Queen of Sheba, was decorated in purple, the score was of C-major chords and the perfume was incense. Later scenes matched yellow with the scent of hyacinths, green with lily, and so on. The poet Paul Fort remembered that 'the projections changed colour with each change of scene and followed the various degrees of emotion rhythmically, while all the sweet scents flowed out.' They flowed a little too abundantly for some of the audience, who found them nauseous, and the work had a very short run.

Another quasi-Symbolist scheme that flowered in the 1910s was the identification of colours with shapes. The essential form of red is square; that of blue, circular; of yellow, triangular. So proposed Kandinsky in his 1911 *On the Spiritual in Art*, and in his great abstract

Compositions of the decade. Malevich picked up on the notion ('I have arrived at pure colour forms', he declaimed in his Suprematist manifesto of 1915), although Kandinsky was departing from his mentor in Munich, Adolf Hoelzel, who had associated red with the circle. Looking back over these whimsical doctrines, and sniffing the banal object analogies (red bricks, blue domes of heaven) that probably underlay them, you might reckon that the whole line of speculation was an utterly daft non-starter. The value of Gage's steady inquisitiveness is that he can persuade you to be patient with it. He comes to his interdisciplinary expertise from a background in painting, and he retains an informed sympathy for the elusive, not wholly attainable objectives that have drawn artists forwards.

As an historian, he notes the actual physical preamble to this kind of modernism: its 'taste for bright primary colour... began in the nursery.' Arguably, the *ur*-objects behind 20th-century art are the 'gifts' that Friedrich Froebel, founder of the kindergarten, devised in the 1830s to help children learn through play: an innovative system of abstract building blocks, some of them brightly coloured, intended to symbolize the fundamental constituents of experience. Froebel's elemental schemes definitely influenced Frank Lloyd Wright, and also, so Norman Brosterman has conjectured[*], Mondrian and Klee. His blocks at least provide a concrete milestone on the winding pathways connecting studio practice and scientific speculation - an elusive network that Gage does his best to map in all three of his books. Previously in Germany, Goethe had tried to outline a *Theory of Colours* grounded wholly in viewers' perceptions. His approach was broadly prescient of later impressionism, psychology and phenomenology, though it fell foul of most physicists. These stuck by the text Goethe wanted to undermine, the authoritative *Opticks*, published a century before by Isaac Newton. Did either impact on painting? It is true that the elderly Turner read Goethe with critical sympathy, and Gage also shows that Newton's spectrum features here and there in 18th-century iconography. But these major theorists of colour sidled their way into the studio by the back route, at best. There is hardly any such thing as Newtonian or Goethean art.

So what kind of a history is there? There are the chromatic resources supplied by science, starting with Newton's 1707 unification of natural light and colour, to be followed by the late 18th-century growth of inorganic chemistry - and eventually, by electricity, film, holography. And then, commencing rather later, there comes a time when those resources seem expressive and content-filled: when artists don't hesitate to read science against the reductionist grain, co-opting cadmium, chrome or neon with full-hearted zeal as if these glowing materials could embody the soul's desires. But somewhere in the course of the 20th century, the hegemony of the hueless - the rule of white and grey, the *Chromophobia* on which David Batchelor published an essay in 2000 - creeps in. The promise of bright colour retreats or gets privatized, and a patch of fierce scarlet here or of vibrant viridian there henceforward becomes little more than a trigger for consumer salivation.

That would be one very streamlined reading of colour's trajectory. There could be any number of counter-histories, of course. In the earlier 20th century, even while Matisse and Bonnard were at their most chromatically lyrical, there was a subversive scatter of wised up, down-in-the-mouth colourists - Sickert, Orpen, Hopper - clawing a poetry out of acidity and dirt.

---

[*] *Inventing Kindergarten* (Abrams, 1997)

Turning to the present day, Gage remarks the fact that technophilia persists in computer artists exploring 'intense and bizarre' colour effects like those produced by thermal imaging. Or turn to a point halfway in between and think of 1960s painting - Warhol, Stella, John Hoyland: is one to describe their use of acrylics as expressing sheer exuberance, or alternately as signalling a complete, anaesthetizing annulment of emotion?

The historical strands that Gage had to consider concerning colour weave in and about one another in complex tangles, and discussing an issue which involves so many appeals to sensibility is inevitably a delicate task. Keeping his assertions in suspense, entertaining all points of view with a scholarly courtesy, Gage showed in his three books how we might begin to chart what the old academicians, with their belief in the linear, warned students against: an engulfing 'ocean of colour', fit to drown any artist. He was that rare thing, an instinctual complexity theorist, roving this ocean's endlessly fractal coastline and staring out to sea.

John Gage died on 10 February 2012

Maria Jastrzębska

BLEU NUIT

These dreams are as common as pigeons.
They settle on your bed, preening.
At the sound of the central heating
or a car door slamming outside, they're gone.

A few feathers remain, grey blue.
You dream everyone elses's poems are more clever
than yours, full of stark images, exotic birds
inked in bleu azur, bleu myosotis, éclat de saphir.

Your poems only contain lost teeth, a car
with no steering wheel, everyday things;
too many bags to carry — balancing
a metal bird-cage at the same time.

Now the wet cat slithers under the duvet
between you and your love, purrs loudly enough
to wake the dead. When the doorbell rings
you stumble down in your flannel pyjamas.

The door is already open, snow blows in
as dead friends and relations arrive.
You offer tea, but the kitchen shelves are filled
with rows of pigeons, their hearts beating as one.

Ros Barber

WHAT BLUE IS

A character's name in all those films that flopped.
The road signs for the motorway cafés
he sits in, writing nothing. Smoke nooses
that used to side-wind from his father's pipe.

The ocean's helplessness on perfect days.
The ink of schoolgirl fingers pressed against
the bare V of his schoolboy chest. Her face
when lights were out, and parents coming home.

The gentle poison of an old tattoo.
The chlorinated pools of movie stars
he may have dreamed of kissing. All the songs
of Billie Holliday. What else is blue?

His mother's sapphire ring. Fifth chakra, throat.
His shirts, since they were bought by her,
his wife. Her eyelids when she's going out;
the coat he drives her to auditions in.

The tell-tale kissing of a recent bruise.
The menu screen. The oxygen-poor blood
in the right of his heart. The woman he used to call,
when he was partly hers, and she all his,

under the lie of having to move his car;
her language when he left her all alone
to curse herself; the shadows of the flowers
his mother picked to decorate the church

where he would marry wrong. A passing van.
A sky that every summer throws on him
for stopping short and giving in; the thought
that sky is not a thing, but emptiness;

what isn't there, is blue. The sugar wrap.
The cup he gets his second coffee in.
That thing she used to wear. The final draft,
when he can almost taste what he has lost.

Mohamad Atif Slim

DIE WEISSE ROSE

Es lebe die Freiheit!
H.S., 22 February 1943

White rose, white
as blizzard snow, as
the papers you filled
with ink, pure nodes
of defiance in Munich,
angry in the atrium that once housed
the oppressive calm. This rose,

white, as though washed off of the
red of blood, fierce at the edge of
its tremulous stalk, a bold slice of star,
a humbling symbol, spread
on my naked palm. O hand, crease
obediently against these thorns, taste
the difficult violence of
beauty — etch this lesson into
your skin, how truth is a
narrow broken-bricked path, but
straight. There is nothing
zwischen Immer und Nie,
only a desert for dying, so tighten,
Fist, onto this flower, its
rope will never break.

White Rose, we are
all sprinters in the same
race, each alike, splinters of
the same drifting wood. Your burgeoning bush
today is bright and lush, your faces
we still remember, clean
between these petals, this blossom

burning yet hot
after sixty-eight years.

14 February 2011

Robert Hamberger

YELLOW ROSES

(for Andrew)

When I trickled the dregs of your ashes —
a teaspoonful washed by spring water —
on the roots of our wintering roses
they hit spiky twigs, a clipped waist-high cluster.
The first time they bloomed I barely noticed.
I was getting through, too blunted and stunned
to register roses. This year I'm faced
with thirty showy blossoms full as a hand
whose tilted feathers edge every petal,
sunning such glows for as brief as they flower
tickled by bees. A tent of yellow roses tall
as you, hassled with air, a fire tower
calling this summer's drag to crash and burn
while I press my thumb hard against a thorn.

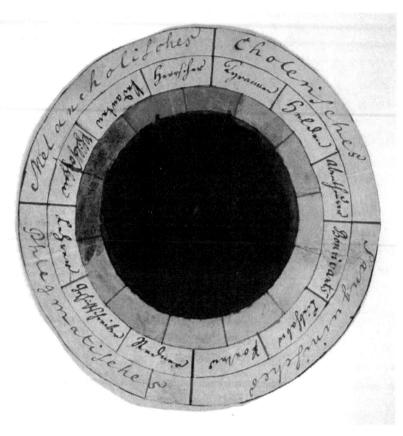

Johann Wolfgang von Goethe and Friedrich Schiller:
Die Temperamenten-Rose/The Temperament Rose, 1799.

Alexandra Loske

TEMPERAMENTAL ROSES
On the beauty of colour circles

The image on the cover of this anthology was inspired by a colour circle from 1799, the result of an inebriated and excited exchange about colour between Johann Wolfgang von Goethe and Friedrich Schiller. Here the two German poets align colours with the traditional four temperaments *choleric, sanguine, melancholy* and *phlegmatic*. In an even earlier sketch Goethe assigns sensual and character qualities to colours, such as *good, powerful* and *gentle*. These aspects of Goethe's research are later explored comprehensively in the didactic part of the 1810 edition of his *Theory of Colours*, arguably the most comprehensive — and criticised — work on colour theory published in the 19th century. Just as this colour circle developed from a conversation so did the image for the cover of this book. Here is the artist David J Markham's account of it:

"After submitting work for the publication I struck up a conversation with Alexandra Loske about the design for the cover. As the conversation ebbed and flowed Alexandra brought to my attention the Goethe/Schiller 'Temperament Rose' from 1799. I think we reached the conclusion simultaneously to create a modern interpretation. I was struck by the beauty of the original circle. What I've tried to do is put a new spin on the circle that has a bearing on the original, the role of the target in art and the interpretation of what became a symbol of a 1960s youth movement. The original circle is paler and less conspicuous than my interpretation. I wanted to generate a bright image that was dynamic and embraced colour, while shadowing the original copy and retaining the words in the correct boxes. Jasper Johns and Peter Blake both found inspiration from targets and this is how the colour circle emerged for me. Alexandra's location near Brighton conjured images of the Mod movement and their use of the target. Isn't it strange how a target can one minute represent the RAF and then the next a youth movement? Same colours — just a different emotional and ideological attachment. That's the story of how a circle became a target."

Throughout history writers on colour have attempted to visualise and schematise the order and arrangement of colour. In many cases the result is a circular shape, sometimes based on overlapping triangular shapes which denote the three primary and three secondary colours. Even Newton, who in his *Opticks* from 1704 eschews a symmetrical order, proposes a colour circle, which he duly cuts into uneven cake slices to represent his seven prismatic colours in accordance with musical scales. Newton's illustrations were *about* colour but not *in* colour, but the later eighteenth and early nineteenth century saw a surge in publications on colour theory, many of which included hand-coloured illustrations.

George Field: *Scale of Chromatic Equivalents.*
From *Chromatography; or A Treatise on Colours and Pigments, and of their Powers in Painting.*
London, 1841

In 1766 the English entomologist Moses Harris offered two detailed colour circles, a re-interpretation of Newton's prismatic order with a total number of eighteen named tints in each circle. Advances in printing generally and lithographic methods in particular resulted in a wave of stunningly beautiful illustrations in the field of colour, culminating perhaps in 1810 in a coloured etching created by the German Romantic painter Philipp Otto Runge, showing us four views of a three-dimensional colour sphere. Flower shapes, and roses in particular, are often alluded to in title and design, as is the human eye; the latter certainly by this point seen as the place of perception, of visual decoding, and perhaps as a gateway to understanding, as well as to the soul. At one point Goethe designed a small vignette showing his own eye under a rainbow.

In England one of the most productive colour theorists of the early to mid-19th century was George Field, who experimented with star and flower-like shapes, always based on a circular order. The only known female colour theorist of that time was the now largely forgotten flower painter Mary Gartside, apart from including a standard colour circle in her books *An Essay on Light and Shade* (1805) and *Essay on a New Theory of Colour* (1808), also created colour blots for each of her proposed harmonious colour arrangements. These blots, although faintly resembling flower heads, are of a stunning abstract beauty. This was perhaps unintended but might have influenced artists such as J.W. Turner. In the early 1840s Turner painted two canvasses with the title *Light and Colour (Goethe's Theory)*. These swirling and almost completely abstract compositions with their direct reference to colour theory bear a striking resemblance to Gartside's colour blots. This is perhaps an indication that artists tend to think of colour and light as circular or concentric in structure and shape, but could also highlight the close connection between colour, vision and the human eye, as well as expressing notions of completeness and perfection. With scientific knowledge increasing in the later 19th century, representations of colour order change dramatically, but among artists and 'colourmen' (producers and suppliers of pigments and paints) the circle, or variations on it, survives, as can be seen in the example of a standard painting manual from the early 20th century at the beginning of this book. By commissioning a modern take on a colour circle from 1799 I was hoping to continue the tradition of beautiful, if highly unscientific, representations of colour.

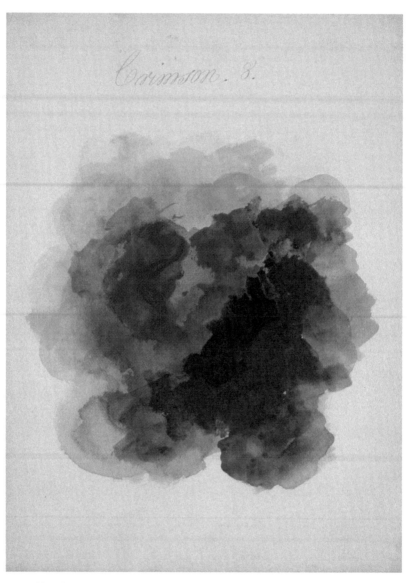

Mary Gartside: *Crimson*. From *An Essay on Light and Shade*. London, 1805

Antony Johae

COULEURS D'AUTOMNE

Il est Novembre.
Les nuages gris
Traversent le ciel
Comme la fumée.
Les champs sont verts
Après l'été brun.
Les arbres sont bruns
Comme les champs en été.
Mais il est Novembre.
Le ciel est gris
Les champs sont verts
Les arbres sont bruns.
Mais tous cela changera.
La neige viendra
Et le ciel, les champs,
Et les arbres seront tous blancs.

Georg Trakl

DER SCHLAF

1. Fassung

Getrost ihr dunklen Gifte
Erzeugend weißen Schlaf
Einen höchst seltsamen Garten
Dämmernder Bäume
Erfüllt von Schlangen, Nachtfaltern,
Fledermäusen;
Fremdling dein jammervoller Schatten
Schwankt, bittere Trübsal
Im Abendrot!
Uralt einsame Wasser
Versanken im Sand.

Weiße Hirsche am Nachtsaum
Sterne vielleicht!
Gehüllt in Spinnenschleier
Schimmert toter Auswurf.
Eisernes Anschaun.
Dornen umschweben
Den blauen Pfad ins Dorf,
Ein purpurnes Lachen
Den Lauscher in leerer Schenke.
Über die Diele
Tanzt mondesweiß
Des Bösen gewaltiger Schatten

Georg Trakl

SLEEP
translated by Aprilia Zank

1st version

Alas, you dark venoms
Fathering white sleep
A garden, most weird
Crepuscular trees
Swarming with serpents,
Ghost moths, bats;
Stranger, your wailful shadow
Falters, bitter affliction
In the twilight!
Immemorial lonesome waters
Vanished into sand.

White deer on the fringe of night
Stars maybe!
Deathly excretion shimmers
Veiled in spider lace.
Adamant gaze.
Thorns hovering
Above the blue path to the village,
A scarlet laughter
The lurker in the empty dive.
Over the floorboard
Dances moonwhite
The Evil's awesome shadow

Arthur Rimbaud

VOYELLES

A noir, **E** blanc, **I** rouge, **U** vert, **O** bleu: voyelles,
Je dirai quelque jour vos naissances latentes:
A, noir corset velu des mouches éclatantes
Qui bombinent autour des puanteurs cruelles,

Golfes d'ombre ; **E**, candeur des vapeurs et des tentes,
Lances des glaciers fiers, rois blancs, frissons d'ombelles;
I, pourpres, sang craché, rire des lèvres belles
Dans la colère ou les ivresses pénitentes;

U, cycles, vibrements divins des mers virides,
Paix des pâtis semés d'animaux, paix des rides
Que l'alchimie imprime aux grands fronts studieux;

O, suprême Clairon plein des strideurs étranges,
Silence traversés des Mondes et des Anges:
— **O** l'Oméga, rayon violet de Ses Yeux! —

Arthur Rimbaud

VOWELS
translated by Jeremy Page

A black, E white, I red, U green, O blue: vowels,
One day I'll speak of your obscure origins:
A, black velvet bodice of brilliant flies
Buzzing around the cruel stench of amanita,

Gulfs of shade; E, candour of vapours and pavilions,
Lances of proud glaciers, white kings, frissons of cow parsley;
I, purples, spat out blood, the smiles of beautiful lips
In anger or remorseful intoxication;

U, waves, divine shuddering of viridian seas,
Peace of pastures sown with animals, peace of furrows
Printed on broad studious brows by alchemy;

O, sublime Clarion full of strange stridors,
Silences crossed by Worlds and Angels;
O the Omega, the violet brilliance of Her Eyes!

Arthur Rimbaud

VOWELS
a version by Robert Hamberger

Black A, white E, red I, green U, blue O: vowels.
One day I'll brag your smuggled births.
A's black busk is furred by brilliant flies
dizzy around a stink, this gulf of shadows.

E's a tent of snow, fog breath,
three glacier javelins hurled at winter's kings.
I spits blood; the laugh on lips
from any sorry drunk's a splashed magenta.

U's green ocean circles every coast,
each tide a grassy pasture, jade wrinkles
on a forehead caged by thought.

O the bugle's final note
fades to silence blue as omega,
that violet light caught in my lover's eyes.

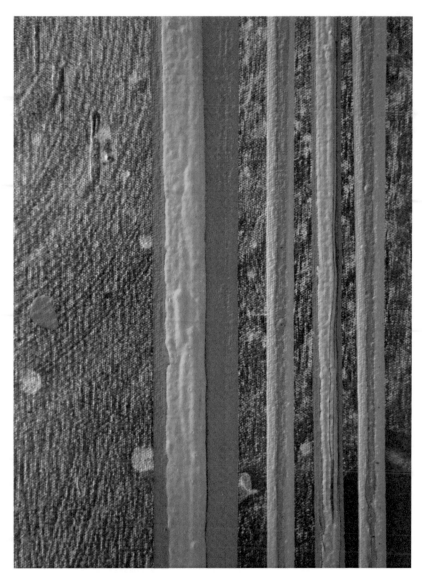

John Hoyland: Detail from *Bouquet for Vincent*, 2006

Ian Ritchie

ON JOHN HOYLAND (1934 – 2011)
"Colour is like love, it chooses you." John Hoyland

I live with some of John Hoyland's paintings. They are fugitive images that evoke worlds other than the physical ones that we have been taught exist. They imitate nothing and I cannot walk past them without looking. They are deep. When I look I feel I am privately interviewing John, not with questions and words or through conversation, but soul to soul – a language of the spirit. There appears to be no difference between his life in colour and his paintings. He seemed to exist to paint.

I visited his studio for the first time just three years ago, and I saw the evidence of a creative journey compressed into those boards beneath his feet, his shoes walking through his past self, on his own memories and travails. Outside, below is a railway cutting and a squint of the London sky above. This was an urban studio, not a romantic studio bathed in light. His notebooks were his aide memoire — containing both visual impressions alongside his own, and others' written thoughts. He was an incisive writer.

John Hoyland's paintings are a celebration of colour — the life and the language of colour through which we see the world — colours that coexist, jostle, some that live with each other easily, and others that appear unable to be together but cannot be apart either. It is a tension that gave the energy to John's work.

In recent paintings, the void, near the centre, occupies an infinity into which one can dive, discover the beauty of emptiness, and float. Then the eye can settle, as a butterfly might, upon a flying fragment within the painting — a glorious moment to feast on blue, orange and yellow, or red, white, black and yellow. These fragments seem as free inside the painting as the butterfly or bird or fish outside; and then imagine the musical journey deep into blue space, or trace a line, gloriously thick, round, red.

It is Hoyland's use of colours that will resonate forever. Hans Hofmann, a particular inspiration to Hoyland, wrote, "In nature, light creates the color. In the picture, color creates the light." Hoyland sensed the utter joy of life, and his maturity allowed him the freedom to value and select carefully from his instincts and emotional knowledge. He recognised and admired this in the work of Picasso, Matisse and Miro. They were not handicapped by style or ideas.

When I first saw his work in his studio I sensed a free man, yet without knowing it he was scrapping with death and that a short while later he would have major heart surgery. When I knew I wrote him a letter about how his work mattered in our thin age. He told me that sensations come from without, and emotions from within. His paintings are translations of his take on the sensations of our world reconstructed by his brain filtering his instincts. Hoyland was at his best at the end of his life. He may have always been at his best.

Shortly before he died he told me that he'd like to be able to paint anything. Hoyland could and he did.

The JOY OF COLOUR

H·&·J·PILLANS·&·WILSON·PRINTERS·EDINBURGH

A flyer from c. 1920 by H & J Pillans & Wilson Printers, one of the earliest printing firms in Scottish history. In the 1920s the firm was promoting the then still expensive use of colour in printing as an antidote to the dark years of WW1, making a strong argument for colours affecting mood. The reverse of the flyer reads:

'The gloom of the war years more than ever emphasises the call of the public for Colour — the great reading public who every publisher wishes to influence. Present your wares to them in warm, pulsating colour tones that attract, interest, and arouse the "possessive" feeling in regard to your books and other literature. Colour in printed matter strikes a responsive chord in the minds of recipients. It influences them favourably, and secures that definite degree of attention which produces sales — an attractive colour-jacket, for instance.'

Trevor Pateman

COLOUR DEGREE ZERO

In his first book of essays, *Le Degré Zéro de L'Écriture*, published in 1953, Roland Barthes introduces the notion of 'writing at the zero degree' and uses it to place the work of Albert Camus in *L'Étranger*. It is writing which seeks to escape both living languages and literary language. On the one hand, it seeks to avoid the 'Naturalism' which copies everyday vernacular into literature. On the other, it seeks to avoid markers of literary Style, such as the preterite, a tense which Barthes describes as 'the cornerstone of Narration' and which 'always signifies the presence of Art'.

On a couple of occasions, Barthes describes writing at the zero degree as 'colourless', thus using a visual metaphor to characterise a style of writing.

But what is colourless? And when something is colourless, is that the same as colour at the zero degree, unmarked both by Nature and by Art?

A liquid is 'colourless' when it is clear and we can see through it as if it was not there. 'Colourless' here functions in the same way as 'Odourless'. But a colourless person is not a person we can see through. It is someone who is dull - or to use the colour word which means the same as dull - it is someone who is drab.

So is it Drab which is colour at the zero degree?

Not according to estate agents. A desirable apartment is one which is 'neutrally decorated' and that means white or, better, Magnolia. Magnolia does not copy from Nature, which has too many colours for comfort, and it avoids previous Styles of interior decoration. Magnolia is a play-safe colour; with it, you do not jeopardise your equity; in contrast to Purple.

What is colour at the zero degree for a painter? Is it the colour of the canvas (which approximates to drab)? Is it pure white? Is it black? These seem the obvious choices.

Black is sometimes thought of as an absence of colour, in which case it is not 'colour at the degree zero'. As darkness, black impedes or prevents the perception of colour. It is then anti-colour.

White is also sometimes thought of as the absence of colour, in which case - as with black - it is not 'colour at the degree zero'. As a background, it is hospitable to colour. You can paint on a white surface and you can hang pictures to effect on a white wall. White is pro-colour not a degree zero of colour.

The outcome? I settle for Drab. That's colour at the degree zero. When Hegel in *The Philosophy of Right* wrote of philosophy painting its grey on grey he was just a shade away from the truth.

Mario Petrucci

repetition not

merely rehearsed through
you but couched
in your way

secure as
that boulder a
well-worn jewel set

skew in its moor though
far less discernible
your rattled

copying
eager for itself
for all its vigour &

play with variety caught
in brown studies as
service to repro-

duction while
this two-eyed wink
in one barely born pulls

with it your automated
stitch of a smile &
that brick you

stretch for how
-ever small or un-
naturally coloured is

being put in its place
as flesh is lost
in praise

of bricks so
a father with shat-
-tered pate & no farther

than his gate seeks in worm
-cast hope & mountain
aspiration to

unrubble
how one might p-
luck your sweet-shapen head

stone clean & wet-shone
from black-lustred
peat without

breaking?

Rachel Playforth

ULTRASOUND

Amongst the other shades of grey
the one that's just too dark,
an empty space.
The dropped stitch in your DNA
my signature
under your skin.

We're collecting doctors,
spend whole days waiting.
My stomach itches.
But every time a thrill,
these preview screenings,
a silvered image
resolving into you.

We get to know you
in black and white,
our silent film star
lighting up the room.
But when we meet
you'll have red carpets, flashbulbs,
roses, diamonds. All in
glorious Technicolour.

Eve Jackson

PINK

As blood dripped from her arm,
alarm gushed from her lips: poppies, tulips,
hybrids with vivid streaks shot through.
Indoors she yanked anger up by its roots,
shucked muck and mud as she moved from room to room.

Then crumpled; black, white, black,
as someone called for ambulance.
Saw flashing outside, went from floating
in pale sky to swimming in Mediterranean,
blinking, who the .... are you?

She was carried out entwined in Jackmanii,
mouth sprouting more Cardinals
than her family would choose.
An hour of scrubbing and all agreed
pink would have to do.

Roy Osborne

THE VERY PINK OF PERFECTION[1]

The notion of pink as pale red most likely derives from the appearance of species of *dianthus* flower, such as the clove pink or carnation. *Dianthus* is Greek for 'divine flower', and it was called 'Jove's flower' (*flos Jovis*) by the Romans. The name 'pink' (in use since the 1500s) came not from the *colour* of the flower but rather from its notched or 'pinked' petals, trimmed as if by pinking shears. The range of colours nowadays described as pink — from pale flesh-tint to deep carmine — also occurs in varieties of rose. Called *roseus* or *incarnatus* in Latin, pink was considered by the Renaissance writer Antonio Telesio to be 'the most delightful [colour] of all, and very similar to that of the finely formed human body. Thus poets call the lips, neck, nipples and fingers roseous, that is, candid-white diffused with lovely, rubeous sanguineness, a colour properly and commonly called incarnate'.[2]

A fair complexion, blooming with youth, occurs, so it was thought, from the flowing together of the sanguine and phlegmatic humours, or when blood is tinted with milk or snow. So enticing was the blush of a maiden's cheek that the poet Edmund Spenser was inspired to ask: 'hath white and red in it such wondrous power that it can pierce through the eyes into the heart?'[3] In ancient times, women rouged their cheeks with *purpurissum* (chalk soaked with purpura dye) or with *fucus* (lichen-pink from orchil). According to Fulvio Moreto, in his colour sonnet, 'Carnation offers amorous delights',[4] and pink is most sensuous where the skin is thinnest: the lips, the tongue, and the vulva. For centuries, pink has been associated with intimacy and secrecy, so that any transaction occurring *sub rosa* — beneath the rose, or under a canopy of rose petals — was never to be disclosed elsewhere.

In Christian art, a rose without thorns, a walled rose-garden, and the pink-beaded rosary were all associated with the Virgin Mary, who traditionally wore a roseate or incarnadine dress beneath a deep blue outer robe. The rose-pink stresses her incarnation as the mother of a god incarnate — of a god made flesh. In secular portraits, a carnation held in the hand signified the betrothal of the person depicted. When the Christ Child holds a carnation it becomes an omen of his future sacrifice, whereas a ripe cherry betokens the promise of bliss beyond. Previously, the pink rose was the flower of Venus, as was pink myrtle. In her haste to help the dying Adonis, Venus treads on a thorn, and it is the blood from her wound that turns the white rose pink. In Apuleius' fable, Lucius the donkey is restored to human form after eating rose petals,[5] and becomes, one might say, reincarnated — an expression that could be interpreted as 'to become flesh-pink again'. It was no doubt with a similar hope of revival that the Romans decorated family graves with roses during their Easter festival of Rosalia.

---

[1] This was written to preface the catalogue of Barb Hunt's exhibition, 'Pink', held at the Sir Wilfred Grenfell College Art Gallery, Memorial University, Corner Brook, Newfoundland, Canada, 26 September-2 November, 2002. Here, pink means 'pinnacle'; see Goldsmith, Oliver (1773), *She Stoops to Conquer*, London.

[2] Telesio, Antonio (1528), *Libellus de coloribus*, Venice.

[3] Spenser, Edmund (1596), *Hevenly Beautie*, London.

[4] Moreto, Fulvio (1535), *Del significato de colori*, Venice.

[5] Apuleius (c. 160 CE), *Metamorphoses* or *The Golden Ass*.

Of all the generations of artists, the one that appeared to love pink the most spanned the High Baroque, particularly in France and during the reign of Louis XV. After the sober-coloured austerity of the late 1600s, Watteau's pastels and flesh-coloured silks and satins breathed new life into the artists' palette, along with colours called *rose Pompadour*,[6] nun's belly, and nymph's thigh. Rococo pink was the colour of 'kiss me with abandon', the colour of sensual pleasure: *la couleur libertine* and *la couleur volupteuse*. For Marie Antoinette it symbolised caprice, inconstancy, and fickleness. For the artist, it was the least earthy of colours, since all sources of pink are organic: madder, mallow, kermes, cochineal, sandalwood, and the murex shellfish. To the painter, however, even as late as the nineteenth century, 'pink' was 'yellow'. Dutch pink was a yellow lake from unripe buckthorn berries or weld; Italian pink was from quercitron bark. It was probably not until Webster's dictionary of 1828 that 'pink' was first defined as 'a colour used by artists, from the colour of the flower'.

What we perceive as pink always consists of an optical fusion of red and violet light. Pink possesses no single wavelength and is absent from the spectrum of sunlight. It can be considered to possess a 'minus wavelength,' however, since pink can be defined as 'white light minus green' (its complementary colour). A touch of yellow and it reaches out to red; a touch of blue and it reaches out to violet, so that a further remarkable attribute is that it sits so comfortably between red and violet that it offers the essential 'pink link' that closes up the artists' colour circle.

---

[6] 'Rose' is an anagram of 'Eros'.

Janet Sutherland

SEA LEVEL

from one window the castle
from the other   trees
wind in the branches
marbled light   against grey sky
green earth on gesso raw umber white
as if the sea has fallen on us

as if the sea has fallen on us
from one window the castle
on its high point
against marbled light   a grey sky
straight lines to the buttress
where it follows the curve of the hill

in marbled light   leaf green
on gesso   waves restless
flooding through the room
flecked foam the pitch and heave
from one window or another
the sea has fallen on us

Jane Kite

GAMUT

the extremes:
it is bleached as beached bones, gone to powder, or ice,
or dyed black like a dog, like a shoe, like a thief of the night.

in between:
there's the sky stealing ultramarine and the leaves
of the grass, all the green and the pale and the gold
and the earth's own browns
and my brick, berry, fire, blood red.

Katherine Lubar: *Four Colours*, 2003

D A Prince

RED INTERIOR: STILL LIFE ON A BLUE TABLE

1947 — the year when snow
blanking out colour, form, feature
became its own landmark —
Henri Matisse splurged a whole ration book of red and blue.
Red walls, crazy with colour,
cracking with heat; tomatoes fat with sun,
spilling from the pool of a blue dish.

What is not red is blue is gold is green.

Three delphiniums
angle for air in a liquid vase,
and beyond the golden shutter a shaded green garden
throbs with loud summer,
greedy with living, its language
blazing this brilliant primary yes,
dazzled and hard-edged. It flames
with never knowing snow,
never being born into drifting whiteness,
not crying with milky cold
or slush-grey skies.

Instead, this red interior —
already grown up, confident of its own palette —
is steeped in sunlight, its bones
warm and supple as willow,
free with unlimited heat, its red
shouting through open windows to blue sky.

Kay Syrad

LIDL BAG

A wild bush, a wreck in the prairie,
roots strewn like raked hair, or rope;

a red plastic can (unknown) (mute), and
the white Lidl bag with its yellow sun;

white stones on sand, hard and dry;
a layered sky with flying grey clouds

beneath puff white; light refracting
on red hidden in the bush; the shimmer

of reeds, line of light cutting behind
(is it an island?) — and she exploits colour

while I remember my thirst for a pure,
absolute red, my fear when I find it —

its prismatic origin, the way it harbours,
ingests, breaks all known colours.

Gina Glover: *Lidl Bag*, 2007

Tania Hershman

COLOURS SHIFT AND FADE

He shouts, she shouts, the cat slinks under the sofa, the neighbour turns up the television, and finally they fall asleep.

The baby listens from his room and wonders what all the fuss is about. He is too new to know that this is not new, this is habit. He has only been in the world a few months and it has taken him a while to overcome his wonder at the surroundings. Now he is registering events, processing them, distinguishing between his parents and the others, between smells and noises and colours and where they come from. He knows that his walls are blue, and his sheets are yellow and sometimes orange. He doesn't have the names of the shades, but he feels the differences. He knows that the cat doesn't like him, that he mustn't bite Mummy when he breast-feeds, that Daddy sometimes smells sour-ish in the mornings and that when Mummy cries he mustn't join in because she cries harder and for longer and doesn't feed him.

He watches her face and sees the dark patch around one eye shift into purple then green then pink. Then there is a new patch, on the other side of her face, below the eye, and that changes colours too. If he touches it with his hand, Mummy flinches, says No, no, baby, and covers his fist in hers. And he knows that if he smiles at her after this, if he smiles at her any time Daddy isn't there, she will stare at him for a moment, and then slowly, slowly, her lips will move and she will do the same back to him. Then she will hold him so tightly and whisper into his ears, *We'll leave, next week, I'll pack and we'll go to Grandma's. Don't you worry, my love. We'll go soon. Soon. Then everything will be alright.*

Steve Garside: *Implicit*, 2010

wandering about in your streets, deeply disturbing,
not life itself but memories of it — your windows, all blind
Aprilia Zank

Aprilia Zank

PAINTING WITH WORDS

To Steve Garside, whose paintings have been a singular inspiration for these and other lines

exhibition
canvas
made of wood
made of flax
made of skin
made of words
mute
in the breath of forbidden embrace

pigment
plugs mouth
blinds windows
seals scars
eyes
brushed bare
gape into premature truth

colour
peels off
bleeds
drips
leaves body naked
belly scorched
on crimson callous velvet

on the shore
seagulls pick at shell-less molluscs

Niki Fulton: *Butternut Squash Colour Palette*, 2011

Don Pavey

COLOUR SYMBOLS IN ANCIENT GREECE?

'The most beautiful solid forms are ... those made up of straights and curves by using lathes and geometrical instruments', said Plato in his *Philebus*. Then, as an afterthought, he added, 'and I mean colours of the same kind'. What were these most beautiful colours? One recent dig unearthed a marble lady, once dressed in crimson with yellow and black embroidery; and nearby, a youth with flaming red hair. These marbles of almost a century before Plato were discovered at Meranda, near Athens, and traces of paintwork show that their colouring was lavish. Marble ladies cluster in the Acropolis Museum at Athens, and it is astonishing that so much exquisite colour remains. Patterns of fluted costumes are crossed by delicate polychrome filigree and pretty coloured rosettes. There are bright blue frits, brilliant reds and greens together with faded Tyrian purple (from the sea-snail) and plum purples against dusty greys and shining whites.

Throughout the ancient countries of the Mediterranean the art of colouring an image with pigment was dependent on primitive systems of colour-lore that stemmed from well before the golden age of Pericles and lingered on until the last affectations of classicism, after the Italian Renaissance. Colour observances went beyond personal preference and prejudices, having their roots in the customs and taboos of the seasonal festivals with their display of sacred liturgy, the blazon of civic and military regalia, and the colour-favours of ancient clans and factions. Only latterly, in Hellenistic times, was there an overwhelming show of the quirks of mood and temperament.

At times, as at the festival of the Theophania, colour was held in such awe that the very gods could put in an appearance as much through the agency of their colours as through any display of statues. Special feasts were held in honour of the vesting of the gods with colours and sometimes with gold leaf, as with the Amydaean Apollo, and with dyed vestments, as at the Endymatia of Hera and the clothing of the Brauronian Artemis, with the flaxen *chiton* and the purple-striped *himation*. The archaic rite of yellowing or *Xanthosis* was associated with Artemis and the spring; whitening or *Leucosis*, as of Athena Sciras, was a summer rite; reddening or *Iosis* had to do with the seasonal painting of Dionysos and the Bacchantes; and blackening or *Melanosis* was an offering to the infernal gods, especially in winter.

The mysteries at Eleusis dramatised the most primeval of all colour contrasts: that of white against black, the opposition of blinding light against Stygian gloom and chaos. The analogy was between creation and destruction. In the beginning, as the legend went, the dark goddess Night conceived by the Wind a silver egg, out of which Eros brought all that had been hidden into the light of day. The hemisphere of incandescent white light came to be called the *Sol Superus*, presided over by Apollo, while the *Sol Inferus* was engulfed in the blues and blacks of the dark lower regions into which the sun descended nightly. The phenomena of nature that brought about darkness and light were seen as dramatic and magical symbols and a key in the playing out of events in the life of men on earth.

The most striking colour convention of the ancient world was the pure white flesh that the Aegean artist gave the female image. The practice was introduced by the painter Eumaros, who, in doing so, said Pliny (*Natural History*, Book 35), made the first step from monochrome to polychrome painting. The idea had its origin in the distant past. The Great White Mother of the Aegean, for example, was the lunar archetype of various pallid goddesses, including silver Cybele, or Juno of the white-cow image, and the shining white huntress of the night, Artemis. Vestal virgins took the white veil, and matrons sacrificed in white to Proserpine, according to Virgil and Ovid. At Athens white was a symbol of joy as well as of innocence and purity, while black was the colour of affliction.

A black-for-male convention was automatically adopted by the potter as one of the economies of the craft. But it became less and less appropriate with the diminishing regard for women in the immediately pre-classical era. The male athlete had experienced a considerable rise in prestige, a rise that had grown out of the impressive spectacle of the religious Victory Games, celebrated on the sixth day of the Eleusinian mysteries, devoted to the initiation of the boy neophytes. Black was the colour of the left or *sinistra* side of the moon. So, in many of the most lavish ceramics, men are depicted with orange-red or earth-red flesh over a black silhouette. In fact, the red-figure vases of the classic era use the colour of the pot for the flesh of all creatures, male and female.

The concept of blackness was allied with the darkening of the blue sea and sky at night; and it was a cyanine, bluish black that was assumed by those Greek women who believed that the spirits of the dead departed into the blue heavens. After death, the soul cast off its physical body and darted into the boundless blue ether, called Uranus by the Pythagoreans or the 'monad of the intellect'. Black also reflected the melancholy condition of the wearer. A black veil was worn by Tethys to make her sentiments clear when she deplored the future death of Achilles before Jupiter. Aegeus took the black sails of Theseus as signifying failure and death; and the cyanine rocks were the grim landmarks that rose in terrifying appearance above the boiling waters at the entrance of the Hellespont.

In redness, on the other hand, was the Promethean principle of heat and fire, explained Pherecydes the cosmologist. And the red love-god Eros had been born from the silver egg out of the gigantic lap of darkness. Red and all other colours were thought by Greek philosophers, especially Aristotle, to be derived from subtle ratios in the combination of black and white. The light, hot colours were said to be vapours of myriads of tiny flames suspended in the atmosphere, and perceived in the fire-pores of the eyes, according to Empedocles, while the blacks and cold, dark colours were believed to be produced from humid vapours perceived in the water-pores. It was Aristotle who had the notion that warm colours have their origin from the viewing of light through a cloudy medium, and the cold colours from the appearance of darkness through a similar translucency — an idea later adopted in Goethe's theory of colours.

The red male figures, as on the marble *metopes* at Thermos, follow a tradition of daubing all cult images, male or female, with red — a custom which predates painting with black, white or any other colour. Many red things were *sacra*, that is to say, both sacred and accursed, benign and malign, a concept unfamiliar today. Red was as blood, particularly the blood of menstruation and circumcision. The many red stone phalli and Priapic figures buried on temple sites emphasise the antiquity of the charged nature of red. Figurines of the Mother Goddess too are found smeared with red ochre, no doubt as the fiery deity presiding over the symbolically red full moon and the menstrual cycle — from the white new moon, symbol of birth and generation, to the full moon symbolising life and conjugation, then to the old moon of mystery and divination. Black with red bleeding eyes were the Eumenides or Furies; but to call up the full fury of hell it became customary to melt waxes of the three *sacra* colours, black, red and white, and to mould them into the form of three-headed Hecate, Ceres' infernal daughter, who was latterly known as the demoness of the third, dark phase of the moon, and goddess of witches.

The painted picture too began a long evolution which was to have its grandest expression in the fourth century B.C., and again during the Renaissance. The simple red silhouette was heightened with white — an invention attributed to Apollodorus, the 'shadow-master'. After the great painter Polygnotus added yellow ochre to the ritual red-black-white triad it really was possible for painters to become 'immortal', as Pliny claimed (36.12), using a palette of four colours only. This was the classical palette of red and yellow earths, black and white, *austere* pigments as against the *florid* dye-colours. Yet it was capable of depicting every nuance of sensuality, from the warm carnations of flesh to the cold reflections on exotic fruit, as well as delicate pastoral tints and the variegation of stone, from the warm, golden patina of Pentelic marble, the reddish stone from Piraeus, to the bluish Hymettan marble, or dark limestone from Eleusis.

In the colouring of their images it eventually became possible for the Greeks to indicate not only the sexes but also between the shades of *temperamental* pigmentation. Since Hippocrates expounded on colours of the humours, or bodily fluids, his doctrine had become so popularised that it was said that the glowing skin of Apollo, for instance, consisted of a balanced complexion of the redness of blood, the whiteness of phlegm, the blackness of black bile, and the citrine of yellow bile. It is easy to see how liquid paints were believed to possess something of the same essence as the humours, which were supposed, by excess secretion of one or other of them, to bring about all the variants of the four chief personality types, the *sanguine* or the ruddy and jovial, the pallid or white of the *phlegmatic*, the jaundiced or yellow *choleric*, and the black *melancholic*.

Two Greek colour circles, the jinx wheel and the wheel of Ixion, were entirely concerned with the passions of love. The jinx wheel was a coloured disc with a serrated edge and was whirled on a loop of string which passed through two holes near the centre and wound up on either side. Its main purpose was to work an enchantment that would restore the affections of a bored lover, 'able to entice a man over the distant sea and a boy from his modest bedroom' (Asclepiades, 5.205). The changing colours of the disc were compared with the play of colours on the neck of the wry-necked woodpecker (*lynx torquilla*) which symbolised the restless movement of the emotions of love; and the pearly, changing hues were said to be caused by the mating instinct which was thought to excite the bird to madness (Pindar, *Pythian*, 212-14).

Illustrations of the jinx wheel on vases and jewels have a woodpecker spread-eagled across it, attached by wings and talons. The colours of the first whirling 'love-discs' are unknown, but on a Campanian amphora from Cumae, now in Berlin, a wheel of Ixion has rims of red, white and black. Ixion, incidentally, was chained to a flame-propelled wheel to screw his way through space for ever as a punishment for seducing Zeus' wife Hera. Naturalists will know that the colours of the wry-necked woodpecker are rusty greyish colours, very much as if mixed from the four-colour or tetrachrome palette. All the same, it would seem unlikely that the jinx colours were other than those on Ixion's wheel — red, white and black, Hecate's colours. Hecate is, in fact, evoked by Theocritus while using the jinx wheel (*Idylls*, 2.17). If one spins a disc painted with such colours, depending on their proportions, they ultimately to fuse into a faint reddish purple — a colour that more often than not in Greek culture had both erotic and divine connotations. The priests of the fertility mysteries of Eleusis wore long purple robes, and sculptures of Hermes, the god of change, were crowned by youths with purple flowers, a colour said to promote puberty. There is much to suggest that the pearly, purplish-red appearance of human blood beneath the thinnest layers of skin made up the classical purple *sacra*. The nickname 'the purple one' or 'reddened one' (*phoinikistes*) was given to a person who indulged in the vices of the Phoenicians and Lesbians. The word is from *phoinisso*, to redden, stimulate or make sore by friction. The same root gives the name of the phoenix palm and the mythical firebird, the phoenix, the symbol of regeneration that rises from its own ashes.

Titillating colours, those which depended for their attraction on what was called the 'itch of desire', were not acceptable to Plato. Nor would he have agreed with Aristotle that the simplest outline of a human body was preferable to an array of colours. Plato's vision of beautiful colours may well have harked back to the religious colours of archaic sculpture. This aspect of Platonic teaching stemmed from his *Timaeus* and led to the vivid and magical symbolism of the colours of the zodiac and celestial bodies, which even now play a part in contemporary culture. What Plato really meant was ultimately best explained by the philosopher Plotinus in his *Enneads* (5.8). Sure, colour cannot in essence acquire beauty through harmonic symmetry. It cannot be generated with lathes or geometrical instruments. But the same intelligence that draws out and designs with shapes and forms is no less important in arranging and tempering the colours. Beauty of colouring is the result of superhuman sensibility and super-intelligence over from, as it were, a super-real reservoir of pure concepts; for art, Plotinus thought, is not a copying of nature but an ascending to the principles on which nature is built. 'These things', said Plato, 'are not beautiful relatively like other things, but always and naturally and absolutely'.

Roy Osborne

ANTONIO TELESIO'S COLOUR DICTIONARY (1528)

In 1528, the first humanist book on colour was published in Venice by the Calabrian poet, scholar and orator Antonio Telesio (Antonius Thylesius, 1482-1534). The only previous Renaissance book wholly on the subject was *Le blason des couleurs*, compiled in Naples about 1450 by an author signing himself the Sicily Herald, and since identified as Jehan Courtois of Enghien in Flanders. Whereas Jehan's book drew on the symbolism of medieval heraldry and alchemy, Telesio's references are all from ancient Greek or Roman literature.

From his principal biographer, Francesco Danièle (1740-1812), we learn that, as a student in Cosenza, Telesio 'made such progress towards the shrine of the Muses that he surpassed those older than himself, as well as far outstripping his contemporaries'. For a number of years, after 1517, he taught in Milan, returning south owing to the threat of invasion by Charles V's forces, only to be caught up in the devastating Sack of Rome in 1527. Rather than return to Milan or Cosenza, 'for fear of being overwhelmed in a renewed assault', he fled to Venice, where he published his *Libellus de coloribus* soon after. Previous works had included a reference book on wreaths and garlands, *De coronis* (1525), and a complete collection of Horace's poems, *Q. Horatii Flacci ... omnia poemata* (1525), annotated by prominent scholars, including Erasmus.

At the start of his 'Booklet on colours', Telesio makes it clear that 'I am not writing for painters, nor the philosopher, but for the philologist who studiously seeks elegance in his Latin prose'. In the following thirteen chapters, he then clarifies the meaning of some 150 Latin colour terms employed by such writers as Aristotle, Virgil, Cicero, Horace, Ovid, Varro and Sallust. The first dozen chapter-headings categorise colours in the following sequence: *Cœruleus* (blue), *Cæsius* (grey), *Ater* (black), *Albus* (white), *Pullus* (brown), *Ferrugineus* (orange), *Rufus* (orange-red), *Ruber* (deep red), *Roseus* (pink), *Puniceus* (purple), *Fulvus* (yellow) and *Viridis* (green).

'First I begin with coeruleous,' he writes, and, 'indeed, if Nature did not take exceptional pleasure in it, she would never have bestowed it upon the home of the gods, which, within its encircling embrace, so joyfully encompasses the universe. Then come the rest in sequence'. Always keen on etymology, Telesio tells us that the term is from the Latin for celestial, and that, since the sea 'reflects the brilliance of the sky', it can also be used to describe the sea. Hence it was the custom to wrap Homer's *Odyssey*, 'which tells of the sea-wanderings of Ulysses', with blue, whereas the *Iliad,* 'owing to the slaughter spoken of therein', was wrapped in blood-red. He also lists *cyaneus* (sky-blue) and *venetus*, a dull sea-blue (venet) 'now commonly called *blavus*'. Chapter 2 informs us that *cæsius* was applied by the ancients 'to eyes that were horrendous to look upon', that is, cold grey eyes, including the eyes of lions. Telesio traces its origin to the verb *cædo*, meaning 'to cut' or 'to slay', as in the name 'Caesar'. Hence, 'because it was said that Minerva took delight in war and slaughter, I think this is why the ancients nicknamed her *Cæsius*'. Other sources imply a metallic glint, 'shown also by Cicero, who said of Cataline that with his cutting glance he marks each one of us for slaughter'.

Chapter 3 groups *ater* (atrous) and *niger* (nigrous), two common terms for black, with other, rarer words, including *anthracinus, furnus* and *lividus*. For Telesio, *ater* is a horrible colour, identifying 'black days' (*atra dies*), and he notes that 'such days of mourning were marked on the calendar with charcoal, whereas joyful days were marked with gypsum'. Distinguishing matt *ater* from shiny *niger*, he describes the first as 'horrendous, sad, unpleasant to look upon, and suited to mourners', whereas the second 'is sometimes charming and attractive, as human eyes often are'. *Anthracinus* is coal-black, from the Greek *ánthrákinos*, *furnus* is furnace-black or 'sooty', while *lividus* might be translated as 'black and blue', so that 'those envious of the belongings of others are sometimes described as livid, as though they had been bruised by whipping'.

The commonest term for white is *albus*, which is nowhere 'found brighter than in snow'. Its Greek origin is *álphós*, the 'Alpine' colour. *Candidus* is distinguished from *candens*, the first meaning 'pure white' and the second 'white hot', hence the skin of Venus can be described as 'candid', whereas 'iron beaten by the blacksmith' is 'candent'. Among other whites, *canus* (hoary) 'properly describes the hair and beards of the elderly', *eburneus* means ivory, *niveus* (from the Greek *niphóeis*) means snowy, and *lacteus* (from *galáktinos*) means milky, linking the English 'galaxy' and the Milky Way.

In Chapter 5, the Latin *pullus*, from the Greek *pellós*, describes drab earthy brown. With reference to Varro's 'On Farming' (3.12.5), Telesio tells us that 'the back of the hare is pullous; and prompted by its instincts and experience, it seeks out newly ploughed earth, and lies flatly upon it, with no part of itself hidden. In this way, and greatly benefitting from its colour, it commonly escapes the notice of the huntsmen, and even the dogs as they pass, keenly on the scent.' In the next section, the term *ferrugineus* describes the orange of 'iron that has rusted for a long time'. Referring to Hyacinthus, accidentally killed by Apollo during a discus-throwing contest, Telesio notes that 'hyacinths were called ferrugineous by Virgil (*Georgics*, 4.183), because Apollo, 'lamenting the youth he so tragically killed, inscribed on their petals an epitaph, as a perpetual monument to his tears'.

As in English, a large number of Latin terms distinguish various reds. Telesio lists some three dozen, including two terms for ginger. Hence 'The hair of the bronze-bearded was sometimes called *rufus*, and sometimes *rutilus*, which is the same thing'; and 'Dogs sacrificed by the Roman priests, to placate the Dog Stars, the enemies of the crops, were described as *rufus*, or *rutilus*' – a reference to the rising of the Dog Stars in August, heralding the 'dog days' of high summer, the danger of drought and of dogs running mad. A man's complexion can also be described as *burrhus* 'when he has dined and drunk well' — a term corresponding to the Greek *purros*, meaning 'glowing-red' or 'inflamed'. Red grapes are described as *rubeus*, and 'Country folk have their own words, unheard of by many town folk: they speak of a *russus* [russet] horse when it is not exactly *russeus*, but a little less red, though it may look close'.

The next caption, *Ruber*, is likened both to 'the blood of living creatures' and to cloth dyed with *coccum* or *granum* – literally 'berry' or 'grain' and referring to the crimson residue of the kermes insect – itself named from the Arabic *qirmiz*, meaning 'worm'. Telesio also places *purpureus* with the deep reds, specifically the colour of the costly dye from murex sea-whelks. And 'not to be overlooked here', he adds, 'is the similar colour of vine leaves, called *xerampélinos* by the Greeks'. For Telesio this refers to 'a type of vine that withers in the autumn, its tendrils appearing bloodstained, and hence the name given to this colour'. He then examines the rosy colour *roseus*, deeming it 'most delightful of all, and very similar to that of the finely formed human body. Thus poets call the lips, neck, nipples and fingers roseous, that is, candid-white diffused with lovely, rubeous sanguineness'. Chapter 10 brings together terms linked with the Phoenicians, the first being *Puniceus*, meaning Punic or Carthaginian, also referring to murex-shellfish dye, which is described as 'flaming violet' and lighter that *hyacinthinus*. The second term, *phœniceus*, refers to the fruit of the date palm, called the *phoinix* in Greek, and the red resin derived from it. As a horse-colour, we are told, it is similar to *spadiceus* (chestnut) or *baius* (bay) — hence the origin of the latter as a Greek term originally describing the reddish-brown of dates.

Among the yellows, 'Brightest of all shines *fulvus*'. Tibullus spoke of 'fulvous stars' (*Elegies*, 2.1.88), while Virgil applied it to the colour of sand (*Aeneid*, 7.31). If made duller and darker, it is known as *ravus* (tawny), a term used by Horace to describe the wolf (*Odes*, 3.27.3), whereas *flavus* describes the flaxen hair that 'often adorns the head of girls and boys'. *Luteus* is weld-yellow, the dye extracted from dyer's rocket, anciently used to colour the *luteum* or *flammeum*, a large shawl worn by brides on their wedding day. The final colour-chapter focuses on green, or viridian, and 'Whatever colour *viridis* is, a multitude of plants show us by way of example'. 'Remarkable among birds of this colour', he adds, 'is the parrot, but nothing is as pleasing as the smaragd', the latter referring to the emerald, described as *Smaragdinus* and named after Smaragdos in Egypt, where the gemstone was mined. *Prasinus*, another variety of green (from the Greek *prásinos*), 'is nowadays called leek-green by the dyers'.

Telesio starts his long, final chapter by stating: 'I am pleased to add here an epilogue, to show what variety there is in the naming of colours'. Different criteria are used for colour-groupings in this section, including Pliny's division of 'austere' pigments from the 'florid' (*Natural History*, Book 35). The former consist of the four constituents of the classical tetrachrome palette, namely, *Melinum* (white clay from Melos), *silaceum* (yellow ochre), *Sinopis* (red ochre from Sinop) and *atramentum*, a general term for black ink or paint, in this context usually vine-charcoal. Of the florid colorants listed, *minium* is orange lead, *purpurissum* is chalk dyed murex-purple, *cinnabarum* is dragon's blood, *Armenius* ('Armenian') is azurite or blue bice, *chrysocolla* is malachite or green bice, and *Indicum* is indigo, named after the Greek *'Indikós* ('of India'). Telesio then includes his largest colour category: 16 colour terms derived from plants. In sequence these are *phœniceus* and *xerampelinus* (both mentioned before), *buxeus* (the pale brown of boxwood), *roseus* (rosy), *hyacinthinus* (deep purple), *hysginus* and *coccinus* (both scarlet), *sandycinus* (sandyx-red), *violaceus* (violet), *ianthinus* (jacinth-blue), *croceus* (saffron), *luteus* (weld) and *galbinus* (ferula-yellow), *molochinus* (mallow-mauve), *balaustinus* (pomegranate-red) and *prasinus* (leek-green). Scattered throughout the booklet are some twenty terms for horse-colour, and his final list groups together other animal-colours: *cervinus* (fawn), *murinus* (mousy), *mustelinus* (weasel-brown), *ictericus* (oriole-yellow), *cygnæus* (swan-white) and *coracinus* (crow-black).

In 1529, Telesio published the 'Golden shower' (*Imber aureus*), a classically inspired drama based on Ovid's story of Zeus' metamorphosis into gold in order to impregnate Danaë. Its Latin verses so impressed the Venetian Council of Ten that they offered Telesio a fee of one hundred gold pieces to take responsibility for training the Scribes of the Republic. In the event, he stayed for two years only, before returning home to Cosenza, where, in the June of 1534, it was reported, with great sadness, that 'Telesio has lately been removed from our eyes'. As his legacy, at least ten further editions of his booklet were printed in Paris and another five in Basel; and almost the whole of the text was translated into Italian by Lodovico Dolce (1508-68) and incorporated into his second *Dialogue* of 1565. Apart from Danièle's anthology and biography, of 1762, a selection of his odes and letters was printed in 1808, two years before Goethe included the whole of the *Libellus de coloribus* in his 'Contributions to the history of colour-theory' (*Materialien zur Geschichte der Farbenlehre*), in which he concludes that, 'even if we do not always agree with his view, we still feel inclined to follow him, in order to learn from and with him'.

Natalia Murray

THE BLACK ICON

In 1915 Kazimir Malevich exhibited a painting of a black square on white ground. The square, the circle, the cross – these three geometrical figures became the foundation and alphabet of Malevich's Suprematist painting. In imitation of the 'red corner' where the icon would be placed in a traditional Russian house, Malevich displayed the icon of his new philosophy high in the corner of the room in which he first exhibited it – at the 'Last Futurist Exhibition 0.10' in the Nadezhda Dobichina Gallery in St. Petersburg in December 1915.

Malevich used to say that 'Modernity is not easily contained in the ancient triangle, for its life is currently quadrangular', so he replaced the traditional triangle composition of the icon with his square. Indeed, Malevich's first title for his *Square* was *Quadrangle*, since its sides are neither strictly parallel, nor equal. Furthermore, his first black square was painted with little Impressionist strokes rather than just filled with black paint. He wanted it to look 'hand-painted', since it was such a crucial work for him. One of his students, Anna Leporskaya, wrote that when Malevich painted his *Black Square*, he first 'neither knew nor understood what it contained. But he felt that it was such an important event in his life that he couldn't sleep, or drink, or eat, for the whole week.'

Although the *Black Square* is still considered to be an icon of modernism, the mysterious side to black had appealed to several artists and writers long before Malevich. Thus the best known example of the black square dates back to the early seventeenth century. It can be found in a page in volume one of Robert Fludd's *Utriusque cosmic maioris scilicet et minoris metaphysica* which was published in Oppenheim in 1617. Here the black square is represented in the context of a metaphysical iconography of the infinite. Each side of this slightly distorted square is marked with words 'Et sic in infinitum'. For Fludd this image was nothing less than a representation of the 'prima materia', the beginning of all creation.

In his book on colour theory, which appeared in 1810, Goethe called colour 'troubled light', and found black the most troubling – the surface that absorbs all the colours of the visible spectrum. In the 20th century, black fascinated such artists as Piet Mondrian, who admired Goethe's theories, and Paul Klee, who said that black cannot be rationalised as it represents the 'primeval ground'.

Matisse strove to establish black as a radiant colour with a luminescent quality. At the same time Kandinsky who also liked using black lines in his work, regarded black as leading an existence of its own - somewhere away from the 'life of simple colour'.

So was the *Black Square* an icon of the new Russia? Was it the symbol of the time when the future of Russia was unclear? Can we treat it as a portrait of pre-revolutionary Russia? Why does it still have the power to fascinate us today?

When the critic and the founder of the 'World of Art' movement Alexander Benois panned Malevich's article about the *Black Square*, the artist replied: '*You who are in the habit of warming yourself before sweet little faces, find it hard to get any warmth out of the face of a square... My square is a naked icon without a frame, the icon of my time. You will never see the smile of a pretty little Psyche on my square! It will never be the mattress of love!*'

The black square in Robert Fludd's
Utriusque Cosmic Maioris Scilicet et Minoris Metaphysica, 1617

Notes on contributors

Kevin Bacon was born and bred in Brighton, and has never really left. He has worked for the Royal Pavilion and Museums since 2003, and has held a number of posts, including that of its first and last Curator of Photographs. He presently acts as the service's digital ringmaster, and is regularly vexed by *Facebook*.

Ros Barber has published three collections of poetry, the most recent of which, *Material* (Anvil 2008), was a Poetry Book Society recommendation. Her latest book, *The Marlowe Papers* (Sceptre, 2012), a fictional autobiography of Christopher Marlowe written entirely in iambic pentameter, was joint winner of the Hoffmann Prize 2011.

Elizabeth Barrett's most recent collection is *A Dart of Green and Blue* (Arc Publications, 2010). A selection from collection *The Bat Detector* (Wrecking Ball Press, 2005) was released as a spoken word CD with solo viola compositions by Robin Ireland (Meridian Records, 2008).

Julian Bell is a painter based in Lewes, Sussex. He has written about art for the *London Review of Books*, the *New York Review of Books* and *The Guardian*, and in 2007 Thames & Hudson published his *Mirror of the World: A New History of Art*.

Clare Best's first full collection, *Excisions*, was published by Waterloo Press in September 2011. A pamphlet, *Treasure Ground*, came out with Happen*Stance* in 2009. Clare lives in Lewes, Sussex.

Alison Chisholm is a voice coach and creative writing tutor, and poetry columnist on *Writing Magazine*. She's written nine collections, as well as textbooks on the craft of writing poetry.

Clare Crossman lives outside Cambridge and works as a freelance creative writing tutor. Her pamphlet *Landscapes* won the Redbeck competiton in 1996. Shoestring Press included her in the anthology *Take Five 04* and published her collection *The Shape of Us* in 2010. She recently wrote and performed *Fen Song - A Ballad of the Fen* with Penny Walker and Bryan Causton. She is working on a second collection.

Graham Dean has been exhibiting internationally for thirty-eight years with his work now in many public and private collections around the world. He has also been awarded the Abbey Award at the British School in Rome and the International Fellowship at the Vermont Studio Center in the USA. After an initial decade of painting acrylics on canvas in a highly realistic 'cinematic' style he switched to 're-inventing' watercolours on a grand scale using torn paper which are sensual, visceral, and colour-led and have been termed 'reverse archaeology' due to the way they are made.

Peter Dunsmore has been a dentist and an organist. He remains a pianist. Very occasionally he may decide to write a fugue or even a poem.

Niki Fulton is a colour designer working in Scotland. She specialises in colour selection for commercial spaces and designs home wares for design shops under her brand, 'unifiedspace'.

Steve Garside is an artist, designer, published poet and writer from Rochdale, Lancashire, England. He writes articles for an on-line magazine, keeps a blog and is a photographer and film maker. He studied social sciences at the University of Manchester, England, and works in social care services. His creative work centres on the unsaid and peripheral aspects of life.

Gina Glover is a photographic artist and is the recipient of the Royal Photographic Society's Hood Medal and the Visions of Science Award (twice). Her work has been exhibited across Europe, China and the United States. She has produced three books, *Object of Colour: Baltic Coast*, *Liminal World* and *Playgrounds of War*. She lives and works in London, and Toulouse, France. www.ginaglover.com

James Goodman grew up in St. Austell, Cornwall. He works for a sustainable development charity and lives in Hertfordshire with his wife and two sons. His first published collection of poems is *Claytown* (Salt Publishing, 2011).

Megan Hadgraft is a freelance English teacher who lives and works in Berlin.

Robert Hamberger has been shortlisted for a Forward Prize and has published three collections: *Warpaint Angel* (Blackwater, 1997), *The Smug Bridegroom* (Five Leaves, 2002) and *Torso* (Redbeck, 2007).

Tania Hershman's first collection, *The White Road and Other Stories* (Salt, 2008) was commended, 2009 Orange Award for New Writers. She is currently writer-in-residence in the Science Faculty at Bristol University, working on a new collection of biology-inspired fictions.

Eve Jackson lives in Bembridge, Isle of Wight. She has had numerous poems published in journals and anthologies and has won or been placed in many competitions.

Maria Jastrzębska's collections include *Syrena* (Redbeck Press 2004), *I'll Be Back Before You Know It* (Pighog Press 2009), *Everyday Angels* (Waterloo Press 2009) and her drama *Dementia Diaries* is on tour with Lewes Live Literature.

Antony Johae is a freelance writer living in Lebanon. He has taught literature in England, Ghana, Tunisia and Kuwait. Couleurs d'Automne comes from *Early Poems*. He recently completed *Poems of the East* and is working on *Lines on Lebanon*, *Home Poems* and *After Images*, the latter dedicated to the films of the French director, Eric Rohmer.

Jane Kite lives in Otley, West Yorkshire; a town renowned for its poets.

Alexandra Loske is an art historian and bibliophile with a chromatic leaning. She is also the Managing Editor of the Frogmore Press.

Katherine Lubar was born in Washington DC and now lives and works in London. The main subjects in her work are light, shadow and colour.

David J Markham is a Lancastrian by birth and currently lives and works in North Yorkshire. 2011 saw his *Brits and Mortar* series of prints published by Buckingham Fine Arts. His art is strongly influenced by the punk generation and characterised by an urgent, dynamic quality.

Natalia Murray is an art-historian from St. Petersburg, who is working towards her second PhD (on the development of Proletarian Art in post-revolutionary Russia) at the Courtauld Institute of Art, London, where she also works as an occasional lecturer and assistant to the director.

Roy Osborne is an artist, art historian and writer with a particular interest in colour theory. He is author of *Lights and Pigments* (1980) and *Color Influencing Form*, both on teaching colour theory in art, and *Books on Colour 1500-2000* (2004), a bibliography of some 2,500 titles. He has exhibited widely and lectured on colour at more than two hundred institutions worldwide.

Helen Overell belongs to the Mole Valley Poets and has work published in magazines including *Scintilla, Staple, Acumen, The Interpreter's House, The Frogmore Papers* and *Other Poetry*. Her collection *Inscapes & Horizons* was published by St Albert's Press.

Jeremy Page's most recent collection of poems is *In and Out of the Dark Wood* (Happen*Stance*, 2010). His translations of Catullus's Lesbia poems were published by Ashley Press in 2011 as *The Cost of All Desire*.

Neil Parkinson manages the various archives and collections of the Royal College of Art, London, including the Colour Reference Library. He is the author of a number of publications on digitisation and national collections for JISC, and the book *Poets and Polymaths: Special Collections at the University of Sussex* (2002). As a child, he assiduously filed his extensive comic-book collection in Mylar sleeves and acid-free boards; a later career as an archivist was, therefore, somehow inevitable.

Trevor Pateman was supervised by Roland Barthes as a student of l'Ecole Pratique des Haute Etudes in 1971 -72. He now publishes his work at *www.selectedworks.co.uk*

Don Pavey is an artist, designer, consultant, educationist and lecturer on the history and theory of art. He is author of *Art-based Games* (1979), *Colour and Humanism* (2003), *Buddhist Colour* (2008), *Colour Symbolism* (2009) and *Colour Engrained in the Mind* (2010). He devised and developed the *Pro*MICAD colour-profiling test, and his collection of colour books formed the nucleus of the RCA Colour Reference Library.

Mario Petrucci is an award-winning poet, freelance educator and eco-physicist. His many prizes include the Daily Telegraph/Arvon Prize (for *Heavy Water: a poem for Chernobyl*) and four outright wins in the London Writers Competition. Frequently commissioned by the BBC and the British Council, Petrucci is the only poet to have been in residence at the Imperial War Museum. His acclaimed *i tulips* was published by Enitharmon in 2010, with *crib* (incorporating *'repetition not'*) forthcoming.

Rachel Playforth lives in Sussex where she fills the time between poems by working as a librarian. A joint collection, *Three Voices*, was published by The Frogmore Press in 2004 and she is currently working on her first solo collection.

D A Prince lives in Leicestershire and London. Her full-length collection, *Nearly the Happy Hour*, was published by Happen*Stance* in 2008.

Arthur Rimbaud (1854 – 1891) produced his greatest work while still a teenager and had abandoned poetry by the age of twenty. He died in Marseille at the age of thirty-seven.

Liz Rideal's major projects comprise wrapping the headquarters of the BBC, Portland Place, curating *Mirror/Mirror Women's Self-portraits* at the National Portrait Gallery and writing *Insights: Self-portraits*.She has projected film across the lake at Compton Verney, designed the glass outer wall and inner sculpture at the Birmingham Hippodrome Theatre and had three solo shows in New York. Her art is held in public collections including Tate, the V&A, the British Museum and the Yale Center for British Art. Rideal is concerned with process and how a plethora of manufacture and manipulation can produce the unexpected, coaxing art from the simplest means; the burnt out bronze cast, the photo-booth strip, oil on wood, etched mirrors. Her latest commission is to illuminate the nineteenth century Whitworth Art Gallery from within using LED light and a projected film of tumbling sari material.

Ian Ritchie CBE RA, architect, founded Ian Ritchie Architects, London, and Rice Francis Ritchie (RFR) design engineers, Paris. He has written several books on his work, had a book of poems published, and his art (etchings) and sculptures are in national and private collections. Among his current projects is a neuroscience centre, an opera theatre, and exploring the colour blue in architecture with the neuroscientist Russell Foster.

Rachel Rooney's collection of poetry for older children *The Language of Cat* was published in May 2011 (Frances Lincoln). She was previously commended in the 2010 Escalator Prize. Rachel teaches poetry workshops for children aged between 7-14 years.

Mohamad Atif Slim is a writer from Malaysia presently based in New Zealand, where he is studying medicine. His works have appeared or are forthcoming in *Harpur Palate* (US), *Nimrod* (US), *Magma*, *Other Poetry*, and *Westerly* (AUS).

Catherine Smith was selected as one of the PBS/Arts Council 'Next Generation' top twenty poets in 2004. Her last collection, *Lip*, (Smith/Doorstop) was short-listed for the Forward Prize for Best Collection. Her next collection, *Otherwhere*, is due out this year.

Janet Sutherland lives in Lewes. Her collections, *Burning the Heartwood* (2006) and *Hangman's Acre* (2009) were both published by Shearsman Books.

Michael Swan works in English language teaching. He writes poetry in a desperate attempt to prove that grammarians have souls. He is the author of *When They Come For You* (Frogmore Press, 2003) and *The Shape of Things* (Oversteps Books, 2011)

Kay Syrad's poetry has been widely published in anthologies and journals, including *Poetry Review*. Her first novel *The Milliner and the Phrenologist*, was published by Cinnamon Press in 2009.

Yugin Teo teaches literature at the University of Sussex. He contributed to the *Creative Writing Olympics Anthology* (University of Brighton 2010).

Georg Trakl was born in Salzburg in 1887. He studied and practiced pharmacy, but also became one of the most influential Expressionist poets in Europe. He committed suicide in Krakow in 1914 following a long period of depression and while working as a medical official in World War I.

Nisha Woolfstein grew up in England and has lived in Spain, India and the U.S. amongst other places. She read English at Cambridge, and completed a Master's in Creative Writing at the University of East Anglia. Currently studying for a PhD at the University of Leicester, she is working on her first novel, *The Impurity of Glass*, about a small twentieth century cult.

Jeremy Worman's collection of autobiographical stories and sketches about London, *Fragmented*, is published by Cinnamon Press. He has reviewed for *The Observer*, *The Sunday Telegraph*, *The Spectator*, *New Statesman*, *TLS* and many other publications. He won the Cinnamon Press Short Story Competition in 2009 and the Waterstones/*Multi-Storey* competition in 2002. His first novel is with his literary agent, Christopher Sinclair-Stevenson. He teaches English Literature to American BA students at Birkbeck.

Howard Wright lives and works in Belfast. His first collection, *King of Country*, was published in 2010 by Blackstaff Press, and a pamphlet, *Blue Murder*, was produced by Templar Press in May 2011. Recent poems have appeared in *The Stinging Fly* (Dublin), *TLS*, and *The Fiddlehead* (Canada). He has won the Frogmore Poetry Prize twice.

Tamar Yoseloff's fourth collection is *The City with Horns*, published by Salt in 2011. She is also the editor of *A Room to Live In: A Kettle's Yard Anthology* and the author of *Marks*, a collaboration with the artist Linda Karshan.

Aprilia Zank is a freelance lecturer in the Department of Languages and Communication at the Ludwig Maximilian University of Munich, where she tutors Creative Writing Workshops. Aprilia is also a poet and a translator, as well as editor of an English - German poetry anthology. She writes verse in English and German, and was awarded a distinction at the 'Vera Piller' Poetry Contest in Zurich.

Acknowledgements

Red Interior by D A Prince was first published in first published in *Orbis* (No. 135, Spring 2006).
Sea Level by Janet Sutherland was first published online poetry magazine *free verse* Issue 16 - (Summer, 2009) and subsequently in her collection *Hangman's Acre* (Shearsman Books, 2009).
Painting the Clay by James Goodman was first published in *Poetry Wales Summer 10*, Issue 46 and in Goodman's collection *Claytown* (Salt Publishing 2011).
Lidl Bag was first published in *Objects of Colour: Baltic Coast*, Gina Glover and Kay Syrad, Foxhall Publishing, 2009.
Yellow Roses by Robert Hamberger was first published in *Torso* (Redbeck Press, 2007).
Bleu Nuit by Maria Jastrzębska was written as part of a 2010 residency at Pen to Paper in Brighton.
What Blue Is by Ros Barber was first published in her collection *Material* (Anvil, 2008).
Illumination by Tamar Yoseloff orginally appeared in her collection *Fetch*, (Salt, 2007).
Framed by Jeremy Worman was first published in his book *Fragmented* (Blaenau Ffestiniog: Cinnamon Press, 2011).
The quotations in Trevor Pateman's *Colour Degree Zero* are taken from the 1967 Jonathan Cape edition of *Writing Degree Zero*, translated by Annette Lavers and Colin Smith.
Julian Bell's *John Gage, Colour in Art* is an excerpt from a longer review first published in the London Review of Books on 19th July 2007.
Don Pavey's *Colour Symbols in Ancient Greece?* was originally published as *Pop Marbles?* in *Athene* Journal, Volume 16/1, Spring 1973.

Images

William Benson, *Principles of the Science of Colour*, 1868 © The Colour Reference Library, Royal College of Art
Adolphe Boucher (attr.),*The South Gate of the Royal Pavilion, Brighton*, c.1910© The Royal Pavilion and Museums, Brighton & Hove.
H. Barrett Carpenter, Colour Circle, 1915 © Alexandra Loske
Graham Dean, *Small Funicular Station 2*, 2009 © Graham Dean
George Field, *Scale of Chromatic Equivalents*, 1841 © The Colour Reference Library, Royal College of Art (photograph by Dominic Tschudin)
Niki Fulton, *Pastels on a Plate* and *Butternut Squash Colour Palette*, 2011 © Niki Fulton
Steve Garside, *Implicit*, 2010 © Steve Garside
Mary Gartside, *Crimson*, 1805 © The Colour Reference Library, Royal College of Art (photograph by Dominic Tschudin)
Gina Glover, *Lidl Bag*, 2007 © Gina Glover
Johann Wolfgang von Goethe and Friedrich Schiller, *Die Temperamenten-Rose*, 1799 © Klassik-Stiftung Weimar (Goethe und Schiller Archiv)
John Hoyland, *Bouquet for Vincent*, 2006 © The owner
Katherine Lubar, *Negative Light Patterns*, 1999, and *Four Colours*, 2003 © *Katherine Lubar*
David J Markham, *Colour Circle 'Languages of Colour' (cover image)*, 2011 © David J Markham
Liz Rideal, *Palazzo Barbarini* and *Palazzo Spada*, 2009 © Liz Rideal
The Joy of Colour. H & J Pillans & Wilson Printers, Edinburgh, c.1920 © Alexandra Loske